MOTHERS & DAUGHTERS

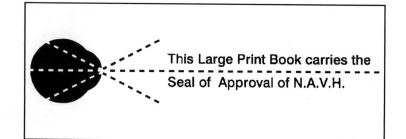

This Large Print Book carries the
Seal of Approval of N.A.V.H.

MOTHERS & DAUGHTERS

AN ANTHOLOGY

DEBORAH BEDFORD, LINDA GOODNIGHT

KENNEBEC LARGE PRINT

A part of Gale, Cengage Learning

GALE
CENGAGE Learning

Detroit • New York • San Francisco • New Haven, Conn • Waterville, Maine • London

GALE
CENGAGE Learning

LIBRARY OF CONGRESS CATALOGING-IN-PUBLICATION DATA

Bedford, Deborah.
    Mothers & daughters : an anthology / by Deborah Bedford, Linda Goodnight.
        p. cm. — (Kennebec large print superior collection)
    ISBN-13: 978-1-59722-968-5 (pbk. : alk. paper)
    ISBN-10: 1-59722-968-7 (pbk. : alk. paper)
    1. Mothers and daughters—Fiction. 2. Large type books. I. Goodnight, Linda. II. Title.
PS3602.E34M68 2009
813'.6—dc22   2009010999

LT

Published in 2009 by arrangement with Harlequin Books S.A.

Printed in the United States of America
1 2 3 4 5 6 7 13 12 11 10 09

CONTENTS

■ ■ ■ ■

THE HAIR RIBBONS
DEBORAH BEDFORD

■ ■ ■ ■

Blessed are the pure in heart,
for they will see God.
— *Matthew* 5:8

In memory of Katie Dunlap,
beloved sister in Christ,
who danced so well before the Lord.
To my daughter, Avery Elizabeth.
To my mother, Tommie Catherine Pigg,
who reminds me as often as we talk
what a gift it is to have a mother who,
above all
things, loves the Father.

Prologue

September 1964

Theia Harkin hadn't gotten a wink of sleep all night. She'd tossed and turned so much that the covers had wound themselves around and around her legs until she felt like she was a sea creature in a shell.

She lay in bed and pretended she was a butterfly, wrapped in a cocoon, in desperate need of breaking out.

She stared at the three-quarter moon, which beamed in through her window, and pretended she could see the man there smiling and frowning, smiling and frowning, moving his face.

Tomorrow, when the sun came up, maybe she'd be too old for pretending anymore.

When morning came, her mother shook her shoulder. "Theia." She said her name soft and melodic, like a song. "Time to wake up."

Theia sat up so fast she got dizzy. She

swung her feet to the floor. She could smell bacon frying. Her mother sat beside her, wearing her red polka-dot apron and wielding a spatula, which meant pancakes.

Mother and daughter gave each other a little sideways hug.

"Ready for your first day of first grade?"

Theia nodded. "Yep."

"Breakfast is almost ready. Come downstairs in ten minutes. I've made something that's just right for sending you off into the world."

Theia didn't want to get dressed too early; she didn't want to get syrup on her new clothes. Her new dress from Lester's waited on a hanger at the front of her closet. Two new Mary Jane shoes sat buckle-to-buckle on the floor beside the bureau, one white bobby sock rolled up inside each toe.

She padded barefoot down the hallway, brushed her hair in the mirror, washed her face, and donned her pink quilted robe. Downstairs, after she slid into her place at the kitchen table, her mother set before her a feast of bacon, a tower of pancakes, and a glass of orange juice as tall and beaming as the sun.

Her mother switched on the AM radio beside the sink as she washed up the dishes. Petula Clark came on singing "Downtown!"

Theia giggled as her mother sang right along beside Petula, spreading sudsy circles in rhythm with a sponge. Once the song had ended, the disc jockey announced, "Played that on purpose this morning for all you kids out there who are getting up and getting ready! Moms, rest assured that the buses are running on schedule. And remember, kids, you can always tell your parents that you are sick and climb *right back in bed.*"

The bad feeling started right then in the pit of Theia's belly. She couldn't eat anymore. She swigged some of the orange juice, then carried the plate, with most of the bacon and pancakes still on it, to the counter.

"You didn't eat very much."

"I'm not hungry."

"You'd better go get ready. Bus will be here in twenty minutes."

Theia padded to the bathroom, stood on the toilet beside her father, and brushed her teeth. She loved looking at their faces together in the mirror.

"Better hurry up," her daddy said, giving Theia a love pat on the small of her back. "Bus will be here in fifteen minutes."

She pulled on her socks and carefully turned the tops down, buckled her shoes, and checked her reflection again. She decided to braid her hair; it made her look more grown up. Her mother handed her a brown paper sack, and she peeked inside. It contained a cheese sandwich, an apple, a package of chocolate Hostess cupcakes, and milk money.

"Thanks, Mama."

"Can you see the road? Is the bus here yet?"

"Nope. Not yet."

"You got everything in your satchel? You've got your new ruler and your scissors? The paste? The box of crayons?"

"I've got everything."

"Well, that's it then. Nothing to do but wait."

The awful feeling grew bigger and bigger in the pit of Theia's stomach. She felt like something was growling down there, whispering frightening things. *What if I have to sit by Larry Wells? What if I get on the wrong bus coming home? What if my new teacher doesn't like me?* Finally, she admitted the truth out loud.

"Mama, I'm scared."

"You are?"

"Yes."

Her mother winked at her as if she knew the answer to some secret. "I'll tell you what." Mama went to pull her sewing box from behind the old tattered easy chair. She flipped open the cover, rummaged through pin cushions and an assortment of thimbles and a jumble of threads. "Ah, here it is!" She pulled out a curl of blue, satin ribbon. Next came a pair of pinking shears, and Mama snipped off two perfectly matching lengths.

Theia wrinkled her nose. "What's that?"

"You just wait and see. Come here."

Theia stepped dutifully across the room and stood still while Mama tied a ribbon on first one braid, and then the other.

Mama straightened each bow with a flourish. "From now on, these are your magic hair ribbons. Whenever you feel afraid of something, we'll tie them into your hair. Every time you've got these on, let them remind you that I am praying for you. That my heart is right beside you. That God is right beside you. And when God's right beside you, you never have to worry about a thing."

"Look, Mama! Here comes the bus. I gotta go."

"Okay. You go. Have a good day. Be careful crossing the street!"

"I will. I promise."

"Love you!"

17

Theia climbed on the bus, and she didn't have to sit by Larry Wells. She got a seat beside Barbie Middlebrook and Cindy Peterson instead. The whole time, they compared tissue boxes and names of crayon colors and how the handles on left-handed scissors were different from the handles on right-handed scissors.

When the bus driver let them off at Colter Elementary, Theia heard a car honk. She turned around. There was Mama's beige Chevrolet Impala. She'd followed the bus all the way to school.

Theia waved.

Mama waved back.

Theia walked through the glass front doors of Colter School thinking she'd never have to be afraid of anything again.

CHAPTER ONE

Thirty-five Years Later

In the basement of the Pink Garter Plaza, the day finally arrived — as it arrived every year — for the *Nutcracker* rehearsals to begin.

Party-scene dancers and clowns crowded into dressing rooms, giggling and jamming on ballet slippers that had grown two sizes tight over the summer. Angels and mice played boisterous tag, weaving in and out among everyone's legs, around the furniture, under the restroom doors. Little girls, with their hair finger-combed into haphazard buns, all wearing tights with knees that hadn't come quite as clean as they ought, running amok the way little girls run in every hallway in every dance studio in every town.

Behind them came their mothers, lugging younger siblings, toting coats and backpacks, handing off crumpled lunch bags that smelled of bologna and greasy potato chips and sharp cheese.

"Angels in studio one."

"Pick up a schedule on your way out."

"Mice over here."

Nobody could hear over the music, shouts, laughter, and voices in every key. Mothers chattered and waved hello to friends. They dodged one another and hugged in the hallway. Several stopped to watch their daughters warm up through the one-way mirror.

"We need volunteers!" Mary Levy, a dance teacher, dangled a tape measure in the air. "This may be the only time we have them together in one place. Can somebody take measurements? We've got to see if the ears are going to fit."

A small group of mothers got the tape and went about measuring heads. They jotted numbers, recounting as they did so the joys and hassles of other dance performances in other years. But after the hoopla had died down, after the confusion had ended and the dancing had begun, only one mother was left waiting outside the one-way mirror. Only one mother stood alone, savoring her daughter's every glissade, every pirouette and plié, watching as if she couldn't stand to take her eyes away.

It wasn't a difficult dance, this dance of the angels. Theia Harkin McKinnis knew each of the delicate, careful movements by heart. Heidi, her daughter, had danced the role of angel last year. And the year before. And the year before that.

A door opened across the way, and out came Julie Stevens, the *Nutcracker* director of performance. "Sorry to keep you waiting. I've been on the telephone. You know what it's like when you get stuck talking."

Muted from behind the glass, Tchaikovsky's music swelled to its elegant climax before it ebbed away and began again. "Oh no. I'm not worried about the time." Theia checked the clock above the studio door.

"Come in my office. We'll talk."

Theia took a seat inside. She folded her arms across her chest as if she needed to protect herself from something. She realized at that moment exactly why she'd come. In this one place, she needed to regain control.

"I'm here to talk about Heidi's dancing."

"Her dancing in the *Nutcracker*? She's been cast in the role of an angel."

"She's danced as an angel for three years."

"Do you see that as a problem?"

In this small town, in another week it would be impossible for anybody not to have heard about Theia's cancer.

21

"Of course there is time," Dr. Sugden had told her in his office when he'd given them the results of the biopsy. "You have plenty of time to seek out a second opinion, if you'd like. I could even recommend somebody. You have plenty of time to educate yourself. You have plenty of time to develop a survival plan."

Even in the dance studio, Theia had to fight to keep the panic out of her voice, just thinking about it. *A survival plan.* "Heidi wants to dance something different this year. She wants to do something more difficult, something that shows she's growing up."

The dance director picked up a roll of breath mints and ran her fingernail around one mint, popping it loose before she peeled the foil. "Surely you realize that we can't jostle everyone around once the girls have been cast."

"I know it might be difficult, but —"

"We can't give every child the part that she dreams of, Mrs. McKinnis. If we did that, we'd have thirty girls dancing the part of the Sugar Plum Fairy and thirty more dancing the role of Marie. Heidi is perfect as our lead angel. Heidi *looks* like an angel."

"She's the oldest one, in the easiest dance."

"She knows the part so well that the younger girls can follow her. That's why we always put her in the front the way we do."

"It is small consolation, standing on the front row in a place where you don't want to be."

"Mrs. McKinnis." Julie Stevens crunched up her breath mint and reached for another. "I promise that I will make note of this. I promise that I will cast your daughter in a different role next year."

There isn't any guarantee that I will be here next year.

Heidi didn't even fit into the angel costume anymore. Every year, some volunteer mom let out and lengthened the burgundy dress with its hoop skirt, its tinsel halo, and its gossamer wings.

Theia laced her fingers together, her hands a perfect plait in her lap that belied the anger rising in her midsection. The only problem was, she didn't know exactly who to be angry with. With herself, for letting time slip past without stopping to notice? With Julie Stevens, for holding Heidi back and not letting her blossom?

With God, for letting cancer slip into her life when she least expected it?

Theia stood from the chair and didn't smile. A crazy motto from some deodorant commercial played in her mind: 'Never let them see you sweat.' She clutched her purse in front of her and gave a sad little shake of her head. "Miss Stevens, someday you will realize that a child's heart is more important than the quality of some annual performance."

The teenagers in Jackson Hole, the ones still too young to drive, had gotten their freedom this past summer: a paved bike path that ribboned past meadows and neighborhoods, past the middle school and the new post office, clear up to the northern outskirts of town. Kate McKinnis and her best friend, Jaycee, leaned their Rocket Jazz mountain bikes against the side of the house, hurried inside to get sodas, and tromped upstairs to Kate's room. Jaycee sorted through CDs while Kate put one of her favorites in the disc player.

'N Sync belted out their newest number one hit.

"Turn it up." Jaycee flopped on the bed and buttressed her chin against a plush rabbit that happened to be in her way. "I love that song."

"I can't. Today's Saturday. Dad works on his sermons on Saturdays. I have to keep it quiet."

"That reeks."

"On Saturdays, he waits to hear from the Lord. He doesn't want to hear 'N Sync instead." Kate picked a bottle of chartreuse nail polish and handed it to Jaycee. "I'll do your right hand if you'll do my left."

"Only if I can put it on my toes, too."

"I'm kind of worried about my mom. She hasn't been smiling much lately. And neither has Dad."

"My parents do the same thing. Maybe they had a fight. Can I use purple? Do you think it would look stupid if I used both colors?"

"If it does, you can always take it off."

They bent over each other's splayed fingers and toes, accompanied by the constant murmur of the music. Jaycee finished with the purple and screwed on the lid. "Did you hear about Megan Spence? Her parents are letting her drive the car already. She gets her learner's permit now that she's fourteen."

"I want to drive, too. Just imagine what it'll be like, Jaycee. We can go anywhere we want."

"Megan's getting her hardship license or something."

"Not fair." Kate waved her nails in the air to dry them and then pulled her hair back with one hand.

"Let me do that. You'll get smudges." Jaycee grabbed the brush, made a quick ponytail in her friend's hair, and clipped it with a hair claw so it sprang from Kate's head like a rhododendron. "There."

"How do I look?" Kate surveyed both her hair and her upheld green fingernails in the mirror.

"Like a hottie. Same as me." Jaycee surveyed her reflection, too. "I bet your parents will be okay. Just wait a few days."

"Do you think Sam Hastings is cute?"

"He rocks. But he's got a girlfriend."

"Well, you know, I just like him as a *friend.*"

"When I get my license, I'm going to get in the car and just start driving. Just take any road I think looks good." Jaycee started brushing her own hair, too. "Maybe I'll drive all the way to Canada. Or Alaska. Or Mars."

"You can't drive to Mars, silly. There aren't any roads."

"I'll make my own roads. Really, I'll just start out somewhere and take any road I want, without a map or anything. Just to drive forever and see where I'd end up."

"You'd end up lost."

"You can't end up lost, can you, if you

don't need to know where you're going?"

It occurred to Joe McKinnis, as he watched the blanket flutter to the grass, that perhaps he hadn't chosen the best spot for a picnic.

Theia stood at the edge of Flat Creek, protective arms crossed over her bosom, counting swallows as they swooped and dipped under the bridge and over the water. Her hair, the same color as the cured autumn grasses in the meadow, had gone webby and golden in the sunlight. As she stood at the water's edge, she belonged to the countryside around her, the standing pines, the weeds, the wind.

I wonder if chemo's going to make her lose her hair?

As soon as he asked himself that question, he wished he could take it back. *This isn't what she needs from you, Joe. She needs you to stand beside her. She needs you to tell her to believe in miracles. She needs you to counsel her the way you counsel every parishioner who comes to your office seeking answers.*

But this was his own wife he was talking about. For her, he could give no answers.

Joe settled on his knees. "Theia? You ready for lunch?"

"Not quite." She didn't turn when she

answered him. "It's such a beautiful place."

"It is pretty, isn't it?"

When she started toward him, her steps rustled like crinoline in the grass. "Thank you. A picnic was a good idea."

"We needed to talk."

Theia stopped beside a little makeshift cross resting against a pile of rocks. Kate and Heidi had made it last year, lashing together sticks with string to mark their dog's grave. Even now he heard the girls' voices, their sad pointed questions:

"Do you think dogs go to heaven when they die, Daddy?"

"Maybe dogs don't have to ask Jesus in their heart because they aren't people."

"This was a good place to bury Maggie," Theia said now. "She loved it here."

"Maybe not such a good place to come today." He began to set out their food. Two sandwiches with ham and mustard. Apples. The clear plastic container of brownies.

Theia knelt beside him, unwrapped a sandwich. "Why? Why wouldn't it be a good place?"

"Because this is where we buried the dog."

She took her first bite, but after a moment her chewing slowed. "I guess we should pray," she said, her mouth full. But they didn't. She kept right on eating. Joe

28

chomped into his apple, as crisp as the air.

For two people who had so much to say to each other, it seemed strange — all the silence between them.

At last when they spoke, they spoke together.

He said, "Kate knows something is wrong."

And she said, "Heidi's going to be an angel again."

"Theodore? What are we going to do?"

His pet name for her. Theodore. Always when he said it, she laughed and poked him in the ribs and said, "Joe, this isn't *Alvin and the Chipmunks*."

But not today. Today she said, "We're going to do what the doctors tell us to do, I guess."

Joe picked a piece of grass and threaded it between his two thumbs. When he blew to make it whistle, nothing happened.

"Of course, this is your chance, Joe. If you ever wanted a different woman —" He looked up, horrified, before he realized what she meant. "I could get big bosoms. Have them remade any size. And I could change my hair."

"You're nuts."

"I could get a brunette wig or even go platinum; no more of this boring, dishwater

29

blonde. We could put me back together exactly the way you want me to be."

"I don't want you any other way except the way that you are right now."

"Well." Her eyes measured his with great care. "That's one choice that you *don't* have."

"You know what I meant. I meant it the nice way. That I wouldn't change anything if I didn't have to."

"I know what you meant. I do."

A Saran wrapper scudded away in the breeze. Neither of them made a move to grab it. "We're going to have to tell the girls. And your father."

"I don't think I can tell my dad, Joe. After everything that happened with Mama, this is going to be harder on him than on anybody else." She started to pack picnic items back into the basket. The jar of pickles. What was left of the brownies. "Maybe you could be the one to talk to him. You're so good at saying the right things to people."

"Not about this. It doesn't come so easy when you're talking about your own life."

For all the things he might be afraid of, he feared this worse than he feared cancer or even losing her. He felt like he was losing his faith.

CHAPTER TWO

The best way to tell the girls about Theia's cancer, they decided, was to take them someplace they liked, to spend one special family day together, before Theia broke the difficult news. They signed the girls out of school on a Tuesday, the day before Theia's surgery, and drove to Rock Springs for a spree at the mall.

As they traveled the countryside, leaves rattled across the road in front of the car. Fields of ripe barley rippled in the breeze. A herd of antelope grazed beside the roadside. Combines waited to harvest, parked atop the rolling hills like guards against the sky.

After an hour or so, the farmland gave way to subdivisions. Traffic began to pass them at speeds that made Theia dizzy. "Can we go to the pet store first?" Heidi glanced up from the game of hangman she and Kate were playing in the backseat.

"I want the music store first." Kate drew

an arm on Heidi's hanging body.

Joe readjusted the rearview mirror so he could see the girls. "Guess you two are going to have to take turns."

Once they'd gotten to Grand Teton Mall, the girls were anxious to go their own ways. "*Please.* I'll meet you at the pet store in fifteen minutes," Kate pleaded. "All I want to do is look at the new releases."

Heidi pulled them in the opposite direction. "There's ferrets in the window. They're so cute. Can we go in and look at them?"

"We aren't getting a ferret, Heidi."

"I know. But that doesn't mean I can't hold one." She disappeared into Pet City.

So much for their family togetherness, Theia thought. "Maybe we shouldn't have done it this way, Joe. Maybe we've ruined one of their favorite things for them. Every time they come shopping from now on, they'll remember today."

"There isn't any 'best way' to do this." Joe wrapped an arm around her shoulders. "Any way we do it, it's going to be awful."

After everyone had spent time in the shops of their choice, they ate lunch at Garcia's. The four of them piled into a half-moon booth with paper flowers in jugs behind them and a bright piñata dangling overhead. The waitress served a basket of chips, bowls of salsa, and brought them each a Dr. Pepper.

Joe took Theia's hand and started. "We brought you here because your mother and I needed a good place to talk to you."

Chips paused in midair. "What?"

Theia had practiced the words many times, but her voice froze now. *What do I say? How do I tell them?* She forced the words from her mouth. "I'm going into the hospital tomorrow for surgery."

Kate dipped her chip and munched it with feigned nonchalance. "What kind of surgery?"

"I won't be in there very long. Just two or three days if everything goes well."

Heidi peeled the paper meticulously off her straw and left it lying beside her glass. "Can we come visit you?"

"I'd like that very much. And after I get home, I'll need to take treatments. I'll need you both to help me before this is all over."

"Treatments for what, Mom?" Kate laid the chips on her plate and stared at her mother. "What do you have?"

Theia glanced at Joe, willing strength into all of them. "I have breast cancer."

Silence engulfed the table. The waitress came and placed steaming hot plates in front of them. No one ate. No one said a word. Until Heidi said what they were all thinking, with a hint of a cry in her voice. "But some people *die* from breast cancer."

"Yes, I know that. But others don't."

"You're not going to die, are you?"

"I don't know, Heidi."

How could she attempt to reassure them when she had no idea what lay ahead?

"Well, I know what's going to happen," Heidi said with sudden aplomb. "Nothing's going to happen to you. It can't. Jesus heals people who are sick."

"Sometimes."

"When they believe enough, He does. It happened to everybody in the Bible."

"We just have to trust that He's doing this because it works for our good."

How can something like this work for good? They're my daughters. They need me.

Lip service, all of it. When it came to trusting God right now, Theia knew that neither she nor Joe stood a chance. Ever since her diagnosis, she'd awakened every night, doubts assailing her, loneliness cutting into her, fear calling out to her from the dark corners of her bedroom.

A Scripture came to her from out of nowhere: "He who doubts is like a wave of the sea, blown and tossed by the wind. He

34

is a double-minded man, unstable in all he does."

I don't want to doubt, Father. I don't want to be double-minded. But I can't be something that I'm not.

They didn't discuss cancer again during the meal. The waitress came to check on them. "Is your food okay?" she asked.

"It's fine," Theia said.

What began as a festive occasion had degenerated to a hushed clanking of forks. The waitress came back and took their plates away, still half full.

Kate didn't often allow her little sister to hang out in her room. "Private Property of Kate McKinnis," read a sign that she'd made in art class and hung on the door. "Do not knock. Do not enter."

Heidi knocked.

"Come in."

Heidi opened the door and stood still for a moment, not sure how she should behave being allowed into such a hallowed place.

"I don't want to go to school tomorrow."

"I told Mom that, too. I want to be at the hospital."

"You worried?"

"Sort of. Yeah, I am. Are you?"

"Yeah."

Kate opened a desk drawer and began to organize it. Pens. Lip gloss. A seashell she'd brought home from a trip to Olympic National Park. "Do you think Mom's scared?"

Heidi had to think about that. "No. Moms are never scared about anything."

"I'll bet she is."

"She didn't act like it."

"That's the way mothers are. They act like they're scared over things when they aren't. They don't act like they're scared when they are."

"When has Mom ever acted like she was scared when she wasn't?"

"Remember that time on our vacation when Dad put the pinecone in the bed? And Mom started screaming because she thought it was a frog?"

"Oh yeah."

"She isn't afraid of frogs. She isn't afraid of pinecones. So why did she go screaming and jumping around all over the motel room?"

"I don't know. It was fun."

"The whole time she was acting scared, she had just as much fun as we were. She did it because she's a mom. So Dad could laugh and we would have a good time."

Heidi surveyed her Winnie the Pooh watch

that her mom and dad had given her for Christmas. "Do you think we'll ever know how to do all this stuff? How to laugh? How to know when it's not right to laugh at all?"

"It's hard thinking about that, isn't it? I hope it won't be as hard as it looks, learning to be somebody's mom."

Heidi nodded. And waited. And hoped.

To hug your sister when you're a teenager is a disreputable thing. So Kate maneuvered Heidi into a playful headlock instead. She knuckle-rubbed her sister's head before they fell, giggling and tussling, on the carpet. In the end, Heidi had to beg to be let go.

Theia entered the hospital through the wide panel of glass doors at the same time a young mother was being wheeled out, her arms full of balloons and teddy bears and new baby. Once she'd gotten to the surgery center, she folded her clothes into the white plastic bag printed with bold blue letters. "Property of _____."

Did anyone ever take the time to actually write their names on those things?

Theia donned a threadbare gown, thick socks, and a green paper cap. The girls and Joe, their arms already full of presents, waved goodbye. The orderly pushing the gurney took Theia down one hall, up another, through double doors. The last thing she remembered was bright light.

When she woke up, she felt as if hours had passed. Voices surrounded her, voices she didn't know. "There we go. We've got her. That's good."

A blood pressure cuff tightened, released, tightened, released on her arm. Theia wanted it off. If she could scratch around and find it, she'd throw the thing across the room.

She needed to wake up and she knew it. The girls and Joe were waiting for her. Heidi would be so tired of sitting around she'd have at least ten get-well cards cut out and glued together by now. And Kate would be wandering the halls, begging another soda off Joe, dealing with this on teenager terms, silently, not talking until things were better, when she didn't have to show that she was afraid.

Theia didn't cry until she saw Joe. They'd led him into the recovery room, and here he came, looking handsome, his hands covering hers, the rhythm of the heart monitor beeping overhead, the IV threaded into her arm, oxygen tubes jabbing her nose.

"Hey, Theodore." How she loved the sound of his voice. "They're having a hard time bringing you around, I hear." He held her head and stroked her hair.

There were so many things she wanted to tell him. "Joe —"

"Shhhh. Don't talk now. Just rest."

She tried to raise her head; it flopped back of its own accord. "Are the girls tired of waiting for me?"

"The girls are in your room. They've got it all set up and ready. Heidi's got plenty of pictures drawn. And Kate's watching some game show."

"Tell them I love them."

"I will."

For long moments, she closed her eyes, slipped in and out of consciousness. Her hand, taped and tethered with IV tubes, began roving. She searched for the bandages by feel; when she found them, she touched her bosom.

"Did they have to take all of it? Or did they leave a little bit?"

No matter how woozy the drugs made her, Theia could see the answer in Joe's eyes. He'd been dreading this moment. Perhaps, like she'd done yesterday, he'd been practicing in his head, over and over again, what he should say.

"They had to take everything, Theia."

"It's gone? All of it?"

He nodded. "There was a lymph node

involved. Dr. Waterhouse did what he had to do."

Fresh tears came and rolled down the sides of her face.

"I know, honey. I'm sorry." He kept stroking her hair. "It's going to be okay." They both realized, as he repeated himself for what seemed like the hundredth time, that the words were feeble and empty. "We're going to get through this."

"It isn't fair that my father has to do this twice."

"It was different with your mother, Theia. Everything has changed so much since then."

"No, not everything. So many things are still the same."

A tube led from her underarm, draining fluid into a bottle pinned to her hospital gown. She watched as it filled with peach-colored liquid. Everything ached. It hurt just keeping her eyes open. From behind them, an unnamed nurse began to work. One by one, she disconnected various wires and tubes. "We're taking you to your room now." She hooked the IV bag to a rack where it could ride shotgun on the gurney. "They keep delivering flowers and balloons with your name on them. It's like a birthday down there."

The girls met them halfway out in the hall. Both of them acted exuberant and happy. "That took forever, Mom."

"Mrs. Clark and Mrs. Ballinger came by and sat with us for a little while."

"Everybody from the church is taking food over to the house. Only we told Rhonda Stuart not to make chicken tetrazzini because Dad hates mushrooms."

"Do you feel better, Mom?"

"No, silly. She feels worse. She just had her operation."

"Like the game. OPERATION! Did they take out your funny bone, Mom? I always make the buzzer go off."

The girls think it's over, don't they? They think I'm safe.

"No." Joe knotted his knuckle on Heidi's head. "I told the doctors to leave your mother's funny bone in."

"Very f-funny."

"Is the cancer gone? Did they get it out, Mom?"

Theia reached for Joe's hand, but he wasn't standing close enough for her to grasp onto. "We don't know, sweetie."

Harry Harkin plunged his spade deep into the soil, freeing the root-bound English ivy from its terra-cotta confines. He shook the

41

roots free of old dirt, gingerly checking to make certain that the plant didn't have rot or nematodes, before he settled it with care into the soft new loam of a larger pot.

It always made him feel like praying, fiddling in the dirt. Nothing like repotting plants to make one think about the Father, he thought, humming as he tamped down new soil around the ivy stems. Every so often, a man got root bound. God had to pick him up and shake the soil out of his innards and transplant him to a larger pot.

Usually, he'd been thankful for the transplant.

Sometimes, he hadn't been.

Harry rattled through his array of tubs and tins that fit together in size like the nesting soldiers he'd once played with as a boy. He glanced up and, through the wavery greenhouse glass in the waning light, saw his son-in-law drive into the driveway and his two granddaughters jump out of the car.

Where had everybody been all day? Place had been way too quiet with the whole brood away.

Harry figured he had the best of both worlds, living in the father-in-law apartment the church elders had added onto the parsonage, being close to the grandkids, having his separate life and his life with his family, as well. More often than not, he knew the entire McKinnis clan's daily schedules and procedures, but for the past few weeks, everyone had been racing around so fast that he'd lost track. Dance rehearsals. Girl Scout meetings. Swim team competitions.

It was enough to make an old man's head spin.

Now that he'd finished transplanting the ivy, he moved on to other things. The church bazaar would come faster than he knew it, and everyone expected his annual offering of forced paperwhites, just in time for the holidays. He'd just pulled out a burlap bag full of bulbs, sprouts already burgeoning from beneath oniony skin, when a knock sounded on the greenhouse screen door.

He walked over and opened it, a stack of planters in his hand. "Come in, come in," he said to Joe. Something in his son-in-law's face made him wary. "It's about time we ran into each other somewhere."

"I'm sorry, Dad. I have some difficult news to tell you."

There had been some discussion among the congregation last year that he ought to root his paperwhites in pebbles and not in dirt. He made his final decision and chose dirt. He turned on the garden spigot and ran water. "Out with it then. No need to drag it out."

"Theia has breast cancer. She's had a mastectomy today."

Harry's hands faltered as they moved in the soil. "Today?" A pause. "Come help me mix this, Joe. Make yourself useful."

They stood side by side, old man and younger one, making mud pies. "I'm sorry, Dad."

"You might have told me a little sooner than this. I could have been at the hospital today." Anger and fear caught like stones in his throat. Anger at Joe for not saying something until now. Fear that Theia might have to walk a path he'd never wanted to travel with anyone again.

"We didn't want you to be worrying."

"I wouldn't have been worrying. I would have been praying."

"You know why we waited, Dad. It's because of everything that happened to Edna. Theia thought this would be harder on you than on anybody else."

Harry said it again, for emphasis. "I would have been *praying,* not worrying." But maybe Theia was right. After what had happened to his wife, he ought to be terrified. He turned from Joe and fiddled with the

44

burlap bag, his only means of escape. He handed three bulbs from the sack to Joe, each of them plump and succulent. "You plant these. It's nice when they've got tops on them like this. That way you know which end is up."

Lord, surely you wouldn't take two women away from the same old man.

He had to hand it to Joe. His son-in-law looked a whole lot more comfortable standing behind a pulpit than he did planting bulbs into buckets, but Joe was doing as he'd told him, burying the paperwhites deep and then sprinkling them with Harry's massive watering can. For long moments, they listened together to the *glub-glub-glub* as moisture sank into the soil, the pleasant sound of something drinking.

You moving me from one pot to a bigger one, Lord? You out to show me something about my roots, that I've been sinking them too deep in the wrong places?

It occurred to him that the man who stood beside him had every bit as strong a reason to feel as mad and lost as he did. He turned to Joe. Paying no heed to his dirt-encrusted fingers, he wrapped his arms around the man who, through marriage, had become his son. "You're working mighty hard to hold back your sorrow, aren't you, Joe?"

Joe hugged him back, hard. Harry felt Joe's warm moist breath against his ear. "You're right. I don't know what to do now, Dad. I don't know what to say to people. I don't know what to believe."

"I'm here for you, Joe. There's not much good about me, other than the fact that I've already been through this once. Maybe the good Lord can make some use of that."

Harry hoped so. He truly hoped so. Perhaps some good could come out of this, and not just sorrow.

He'd had enough sorrow to last a lifetime.

CHAPTER THREE

During the past few days, Joe had canceled at least five counseling appointments at his office.

He had neither the time nor the inclination to listen to other people's problems.

Perception, he always told everyone during the sessions. It's a matter of perception. When you see something as being hopeless, it will be.

He leaned back in his office chair and stared out the window onto the church lawn. He'd left the hospital this afternoon because he couldn't stand to be near the antiseptic smell any longer. He felt like he'd been wandering the halls of St. John's for days, thanking people for bringing flowers and food, being useless.

He'd been touched by his father-in-law's response to news of Theia's illness. Where Harry might have railed at the injustice of

Theia's cancer, he'd responded to Joe's pain instead.

Is that what You do, Lord? Use men who've been broken and emptied to minister, so everyone will see that it's You?

It occurred to him that this was the first time since they'd diagnosed his wife that he'd spoken directly to his Heavenly Father.

Isn't there some other, easier way?

He'd gotten so tired of putting on the charade. Theia needed him to be strong, and he was nothing but a fraud.

His secretary, Sarah Hodges, buzzed him on his intercom. "Joe? The church decorating committee is here. They're meeting in the adult Sunday school room. Can you come?"

He'd procrastinated with church business for as long as humanly possible. He'd already instructed Sarah to keep all of his appointments on the books today. "Tell them I'll be there in a few minutes."

When he walked in the room, he was accosted by five different churchwomen, all with varying opinions about the upcoming holiday decorating.

"I think it's a shame we don't put a tree at the front of the church," announced Mary Cathcart. "We used to do that when we were in the small sanctuary, and it was beautiful."

"I don't like the idea of a tree beside the altar. It puts too much emphasis on secular Christmas celebrations."

"We made Christian decorations for it one year. Cut them out of those white trays that they use for the meat at Albertson's and outlined them with glitter. Jesus fish and crosses."

"People like getting married that time of year because they can have the tree."

"I think we ought to put the manger scene on the chancel. That's what we need to emphasize."

"We need to have a Saturday potluck where everyone comes prepared to decorate. A churchwide hanging-of-the-greens ceremony."

"The Presbyterians always do a hanging-of-the-greens. They'll think we're copying them."

"Well, aren't we?"

They quieted down. It became obvious as they eyed him that they were waiting for Joe to tell them who was right and who was wrong.

"We shouldn't copy the Presbyterians," was all he could think to say.

Next on Joe's agenda came a meeting with his choir director, Ray Johnson.

"The youth worship team feels that the Lord is leading them to do a song this Sunday called 'Love to the Highest Power.' "

"It sounds like a good song with a good message."

"It's rock, Joe. I think it might scare some people."

Joe scrubbed his forehead with his fingers. What to do with this? "Can you convince them to wait a week or two? We'll call it youth Sunday or something. That way nobody will be offended."

After Ray left, Joe straightened his shirt. He puffed out his cheeks and let the air go out of them. When Dr. Waterhouse had come to the room to see Theia early this morning, he'd told them everything they didn't want to hear. "Your tumor did not have a distinct boundary, Mrs. McKinnis. We are reasonably certain that we got it all. Not positive, but reasonably certain."

"When can you be more than reasonably certain? When can we be positive?"

"After her treatments are over, if there are no new recurrences in five years — then we can be positive."

"Five years? She's going to have to live with this for five years?"

The surgeon made notes on his clipboard.

"We hope so, Mr. McKinnis."

His last appointment of the day. Joe was ashamed, but he'd been dreading it the most. He walked into the front office and gave Winston Taylor a hearty handshake. He knew what they'd be talking about. He'd been counseling this man for well over a year.

"Thanks for making the time for me, Joe." Winston toted his Bible with him, tucked beneath one elbow of his sheepskin coat.

"Come on back, Win."

He shut the door behind him, and they were alone. He settled Winston in one of the portly chairs arranged in a conversational grouping and settled himself in the chair opposite. He crossed his legs and cleared his throat, waiting for the other man to begin.

"You're going to be surprised at what I came here to talk about." Winston uncrossed his own legs and leaned forward.

"I will?" *Good luck.*

"I came here to talk about you and your wife."

Joe was instantly taken aback. "Theia and I are fine, Win. There's no need worrying yourself about that."

"That's not what the Lord's been telling me, Pastor Joe. Every time I start out trying to pray for something else, *bam!* There I am praying for you two instead."

"That's amazing."

"Seems to me there must be some sort of a battle going on. And it isn't about what's going on in Theia's body. It's about what's going on in your heart."

Joe laughed. It was the only way he knew to cover the pain welling in his own soul, the grief welling in his spirit. "I thought I was supposed to be the pastor here."

"I got a sermon to give you, so you just sit back and listen."

"Okay." Joe repositioned himself in his chair.

"As I see it, Joe McKinnis, God's looking for something specific from you. He wants you to step away from all the trappings of being religious. He wants you to figure out what it is from Him that you're expecting."

"Expecting?"

"Think about it. How did everybody feel when the soldiers crucified Jesus? How did they feel when Jesus died?"

"That doesn't have anything to do with this situation."

"It has *everything* to do with it."

"I don't see that."

"Think what Christ's followers *expected* on His crucifixion day. Then consider what they *got,* instead. A thousandfold more. But Christ had to die first as they stood there waiting for miracles to happen."

Joe slowly began to nod.

"Those folks had to go through the experience from top to bottom. They got all of the anguish, and then they got all of the restoration. The impossible happened. The moment Christ died on the cross, life as they knew it was over. Nothing looked the way they'd expected it to look. Then, an empty tomb. Mary Magdalene in the garden. Some of them so sure He was gone that when they saw Him walking around, they didn't even *recognize* Him."

"It's an amazing story, isn't it?"

"I'll tell you this much, Pastor Joe. What's going to happen with Theia is going to happen, whether you let yourself expect it or not. If you don't get anything else from me, get this. What you *expect* from Theia's situation is going to influence the way you *see* it."

Should he listen to this man, this parishioner who so often had come to Joe for help before? He didn't know. Just because he was a pastor, did it mean he was the only one who had authority to teach in Jesus' name? The Gospel of Matthew said, "You have hidden these things from the wise, and revealed them to little children." After Winston left his office, Joe stared at Theia's picture.

What do I expect, Lord?

This hurt so much. If only he, instead of his wife, could fight this battle.

Theia had had a chance once to be a dancer. She'd gotten a dance scholarship to Utah State. She'd married him instead. She'd fed him and nurtured him through seminary. She had mothered the girls. She'd put up with 3 a.m. phone calls during church crises. She had welcomed her father into their fold, being just as loving a daughter as she was a mother.

Do I expect peace? Assurance that You will heal her? That she could go through all of this and not have to be afraid?

He buried his face in his hands.

EXPECT ME, BELOVED.

But it was as though Joe couldn't hear. His grief overpowered everything else, and he focused on that rather than the phone's constant ringing in the office, the Mothers of Preschoolers meeting in the Fellowship Hall.

And the insistent, gentle voice calling, giving him the very answer that he sought.

"It's okay, Grandpa." Kate clutched Harry

Harkin's hand as she poked her nose inside the hospital room. "If Mom's sleeping, we can wake her up. She wants to see you."

At the sound of her daughter's voice, Theia rolled her head sideways on the pillow. "Hey, you." She shot Kate a little sad smile. "What's up?"

"Just checking on you. Grandpa's been driving me all around town in his old car."

"Grandpa's here? Daddy?" Theia pushed herself against the mattress and did her best to sit higher. She winced.

Harry came to the foot of the bed, a pot of pink geraniums in his hand. "Since Joe came to tell me what was going on, thought I'd better stop on over for a visit."

"Those are beautiful."

"They ought to be, coming from my greenhouse."

Kate took the flowers from him and set them, exuberant and lacy bright, in the hospital window.

"Thought getting that old Ford Fairlane out of the meadow would be a good excuse." He doffed his tweed hat. "Thought I'd best come over here and let you know that I know."

She could guess at the things he wanted to say to her. She knew he wanted to offer simple reassurances, but he couldn't. "I'm so sorry, Daddy."

I never wanted this to happen to you, he might have said.

I never wanted you to go through this a second time, she might have said.

But they wouldn't delve into the past or the future with Kate standing there.

They changed the subject and talked about the Ford instead.

"You got that old car started. With the weather this cold, too."

"Had to drive to Shervin's and get a new battery. Once it turned over, though, that was it. Purred like a kitten ever since."

Kate plucked one yellow leaf from the geraniums in the window. She walked across the room and threw it away. "Grandpa says I can have that old car when I start driving, Mom. He thinks it'll be the perfect car for a teenager."

It was clear Harry hadn't wanted Kate to announce it like that. He had the grace to appear a little sheepish. "Thought that might take everybody's mind off other things."

Theia's lunch came rattling in on a metal cart. The candy striper moved a basket of daisies, a box of tissues, and situated the tray.

"You want something to eat, Kate? You

can get a hamburger in the cafeteria. There's money in my bag."

"I've got money." Harry plopped his hat on Theia's feet and fished out his wallet. He unfolded his money and counted out three one-dollar bills. He was getting so slow, Theia thought. If she hadn't been sick, she'd have taken money from her purse and whisked Kate out the door before he'd ever had the chance to pitch in. Those hands. Hands that had held her as a baby. She hadn't noticed they were growing so feeble.

"Thanks, Grandpa." Kate took the proffered bills. "I'll probably just get a hamburger. Nothing much. You want me to bring you anything?"

He shook his head. "I ate already."

Kate headed out the door, and the moment she did, the mood between Theia and her father changed. He seemed to sag. He lowered himself into the plastic chair beside the bed. "Joe came over and told me everything last night."

"Of all people, I hated for you to hear this news."

"You'd better eat your lunch. It's going to get cold."

"Jell-O is already cold. I won't do much harm to it by waiting."

"You need to do everything the doctors

57

tell you to do."

"I will. I promise, Daddy."

"You get plenty of rest. You've got to do everything that they know to do to fight this thing."

"I'm thinking it will be different for me. They found my lump so much earlier than they found Mama's. Treatments are much more advanced now than they were then."

"You take care of yourself. And take care of Joe. I told him last night, I may not be good for much, but maybe I can steer him in the right direction some."

"He needs that. Everybody depends on him. It's hard to start depending on people when you're used to them depending on you."

Harry rose from the chair and fiddled with the window blinds. "You know what I was thinking going off to sleep last night? About those times when your mother and I used to tuck you in bed."

"Oh no." Theia smiled in spite of everything. "Not this."

Kate walked back in with her hamburger.

"The 'Purple People Eater' song."

"Dad. No. It hurts too much to laugh."

Kate started unwrapping her burger. "What's the 'Purple People Eater' song?"

"You want to hear it?" Harry grabbed his

hat again and held out one arm, vaudeville style.

"Dad, don't." But Theia was already laughing. She grabbed a pillow and hugged it, giggling against it. And that made her feel just fine.

Harry began to sing. "It was a long-haired, long-eared flying Purple People Eater."

"Don't!" Oh, how her chest hurt when she laughed. But it didn't matter. Laughter felt wonderful. "You aren't even singing the right words!"

"Yeah, but I've got the tune down exactly."

"Mama hated when you did that. You always made me scream and act silly right at bedtime."

"I've never heard of that song." Kate bit into her hamburger and spoke with her mouth full. "It sounds way goofy."

"Mama always got stuck with the job of calming me down. She'd bring me hot cocoa and let me sip it in bed. Then she'd pray with me and tuck me in and tell me I didn't have to worry about Dad's crazy songs because I wasn't purple."

Father and daughter shared a smile. It seemed an odd, nice time to be enjoying a memory.

"Your mother was always finding ways to settle you down."

"You know what *I* was thinking about the other day?" Theia asked.

Kate gave a grimace of distaste and pulled a pickle from inside the bun. "What?"

"Something I haven't thought about in a long time. Mama gave me hair ribbons once. She got them out of her sewing box and tied them in my braids on the first day of first grade."

"So?"

"They were just for me. I was scared to ride the school bus and go in to meet my new teacher. And —" she grinned at her dad again "— she wanted me to stretch my wings and go through those things on my own. But she followed the bus in her car. I saw her in the parking lot! She waved at me and then drove off."

"Is that how come you followed me and Heidi in your car on the first day of school, too?"

Theia nodded. "Yep."

Kate threw away the burger wrappings and shrugged into her sweatshirt. "I don't see what hair ribbons have to do with anything."

"For a long time, I wore them whenever I was afraid. Larry Wells told me he was going to steal my lunch once, but I wore my ribbons, and I wouldn't let him have it. Told him I was going to kick him where it counted if he stole my bologna sandwich."

Harry and Kate both spoke at the same time.

"Mom!"

"Theia!"

"I wore them every Friday when I had spelling tests. I wore them in the third grade choir concert when I had to sing 'Fifty-Nifty' on stage by myself. I wore them on the day I had to give away all my kittens and on the day I had to get stitches in my chin. When I got too big to wear them in my hair, I wore them tied to my sneakers."

Harry put his hat on his head and took his granddaughter's arm. "We'd better get home and let you get some rest."

"I wonder where those ribbons went. . . ." Theia settled back down in her pillows, feeling a hundred times better than she'd felt when Harry and Kate first arrived. "I'd like to find them. I'm sure they're hidden away in a drawer somewhere. I haven't seen them for years."

"We'll help you look, Mom." Kate waved as she ducked out the door. "I'd like to see them, too."

CHAPTER FOUR

When the phone began ringing, Heidi raced through the kitchen, slipping on the linoleum in her socks, doing her best to beat her sister.

"I don't know why you're in such a hurry to answer the phone." Kate perched beside the sink, nonchalantly crisscrossing a new Delia's ribbon shoelace into her Sketchers. "It's just somebody else calling to see if Mom's home from the hospital. Or else it's for me."

"No, it's for me." Heidi rounded the kitchen counter and grabbed the receiver.

"It isn't for you. It's never for you. If it isn't about Mom, it's for me. Everybody wants to talk about the car Grandpa Harkin's giving me."

"Hello?" Heidi almost couldn't answer, she was panting so hard. "McKinnis residence."

"I'd like to speak with Heidi McKinnis, please."

Heidi poked out her chin and grinned at her sister, a blatant gesture of victory. "This is Heidi."

"This is Julie Stevens from Dancers' Workshop. Do you have a minute? I'd like to talk to you."

"I — I have a minute." At the sound of such astonishment in Heidi's voice, even Kate stopped to listen.

"Good." A hesitation. "Well, you see, it's this. I'm making a change or two in the *Nutcracker* performance."

"Oh, I'm so sorry I missed practice last Saturday. My mom was in the hospital. I promise I'll be there next week."

"I know all about that. Missing practice every once in a while is nothing to be concerned about. But I do want to talk to you about your role as an angel."

"You do?"

"As you know, Heidi, the angels are an audience favorite. Gauzy wings, hoop skirts, the tiniest floating steps, the youngest most angelic girls we can find."

"My mom tells me that every year."

"I hope you don't mind that I'm having to change things."

"Change things?" Heidi gripped the receiver. "What do you mean?"

"I'd like to change your part, Heidi, if you don't mind."

"I don't mind."

"I'm having trouble with the clowns this year. I didn't cast as many for some reason, and for the choreography to come off the way I want it to, I've got to bring in another girl."

"Oh!"

"Do you think you might be interested?"

"I'm interested, all right! I *love* the clowns. That's always been my favorite part, seeing everyone come out from under Mother Ginger's skirt."

"Of course, this doesn't give you long to learn the part. They've already been dancing it for several weeks. But I'll bet you can pull it off."

"I can. I know I can."

"As part of the choreography, you'll have to turn a cartwheel. Do you know how to turn a cartwheel?"

For the first time during the conversation, Heidi faltered. "No. I don't."

"Do you think you could learn? Is there someone who can teach you?"

"My mother can show me how."

"That's it, then. We're all set. Rehearsal time is the same. Only you'll be dancing in studio three instead of studio one."

"I'll be there. I promise I'll be there."

"Someone will measure you Saturday so we can fit you with a costume."

"Thank you. I'll be a good clown. You'll see."

"Perfect. We'll see you on Saturday."

Kate knocked on Heidi's door. Heidi's door didn't have any signs that said "Private Property." It didn't have any signs that read, "Do not knock. Do not enter."

When Heidi opened the door and saw her sister come to visit, she gestured with a wide-eyed expression. She might as well have been entertaining royalty.

Kate parted the dangling, blue door beads and entered.

"You can sit at my desk if you want."

"Thanks."

Kate sat down and turned around in the wooden chair, gripping the back. Above them both, glow-in-the-dark stars dotted the ceiling. A jumble of stuffed animals filled up an entire corner.

"How many animals do you have, Heidi?"

"Forty-three."

"You counted them?"

"Yep. But those don't count the ones that are in the garage."

A lull came. "I just wanted to tell you something."

"What?"

"That I think your dancing's really cool."

"Huh?"

"I think it's sweet that you've moved up and you're dancing the part of a clown."

Heidi stared at her sister. "How come you say that?"

"Well, I couldn't get up and dance like that in front of everybody. I was thinking about it, going off to sleep last night, and I thought I should tell you. It's bad enough dancing something that you *know.* But getting up in front of the town and dancing something that's different, I think that's really cool."

"Are you trying to scare me about this?"

"No. I just wanted you to know how I felt."

"Well, thanks."

"You're welcome."

Kate stared at the stars on the ceiling. "Do those glow all night long after you've turned out the lights?"

"Not all night. They go dark about three or four in the morning."

"You lay here and watch them that long?"

"No. But sometimes I wake up."

Kate scrubbed the toe of her Sketcher

against the carpet. "I woke up last night. Do you ever wonder what it will be like when we grow up and get to be moms?"

"Yeah."

"We'll have kids."

"Yeah."

"I decided I'm going to keep a journal."

"You are?"

"Yeah. I'm going to write down everything I think about being the mother of a teenager. And then when I'm the mother of somebody that's as old as me, I can open up my journal and take my own advice."

"What if your own advice is wrong?"

"I don't know. Guess I'll figure that out. I'll pray about it the way Mom does. The way Grandma did."

"I think that will be fun, too."

"You know how you feel about dancing? All proud and everything? That's the way I think I'll feel about having kids and stuff."

"Do you think Mom feels that way about us?"

Kate thought for a moment. "Yes, I think she does."

The Sunday before church, it snowed.

A brisk tinge in the air came first and then the flakes, tiny flakes at sunrise, then larger ones, a confetti celebration outside the windows.

Snow blanketed the grass and etched a scalloped edge along the picket fence. At the morning service, excitement from outside carried into the sanctuary. A vast jumble of coats, from ski parkas to furs, hung on pegs in the front vestibule. Snow boots lay in disarray, no two together the same. Folks shivered and laughed and tucked their gloves away, talking about the mountain, when the runs would open for skiing, if the new snow had brought elk down into the refuge out of the hills.

Theia found her place along the pew and tried her best to concentrate on God.

She couldn't think about the church service at hand. She couldn't think about the snow outside. Even though she'd laughed miraculously with her father's singing, she could only think about breast cancer today. Her mind drifted. Worried. Wondered.

Had the cancer spread to other parts of her body?

If it hadn't yet, would it still?

As music began to fill the place of worship, Kate and Jaycee sidled into the seats beside them. "Where's your sister?" Theia asked.

"Oh, she'll get here. She's probably back in the Sunday school room helping the little kids clean up."

"She's probably back in the Sunday school room trying to get extra candy from Mrs. Taggart. They played some game in there with chocolate chips."

One by one, the women sitting near Theia began to rub her on the shoulder or nod their heads at her or wish her well: *We were worried about you. We've been praying. Are you okay? Is there anything we can do to help? We know how you must feel.*

She gave the same response, the same answers to each of them. *Thank you for praying. No need to worry. Everything's fine. You know how it is.*

Lord, please. I don't want to be here. I shouldn't have come to church today. It's too soon. I'm not ready for this.

Theia felt as if she were drowning in the deep, thrashing about, exhausted, trying to keep her head where she could breathe.

Why did they all have to be so sympathetic? Why couldn't they talk about something else? Why couldn't they share their own problems or something fun that was going on?

Why couldn't they pretend that none of this was happening?

Theia glanced down to see a little boy she'd taught in vacation Bible school at her knees. He threw his arms around her legs and hugged her. He gazed up at her with dark eyes so wide and pure, she wanted to cry out.

"Hello, Landon." Despite her missing oblique muscle, her tight tendons, she managed to lift him cautiously into her arms. It felt so odd, hugging him this way. Just holding a small child's body against her wounded chest brought forth a sense of loss that overwhelmed her. She ached to be whole again. The little boy planted a wet kiss on her lips. "I love you," he whispered.

"I love you, too, Landon." She couldn't keep the tears from coming to her eyes.

Lord, I'm the pastor's wife. I'm a mother to two girls of my own. I can't tell anybody that I'm afraid. I have no right.

Everyone around her kept offering advice.

"You ought to meet Jo Beth Mason. She's a cancer survivor. She's doing really well."

"I have a miracle book you can read. All about the herbal things you can do."

"We know you can do this, Theia." This one was always said with a careful I-know-you-can-do-it smile.

Landon's mother came to take him away, and when the next person tapped her on the shoulder, she turned again, expecting another embrace.

Instead she came face-to-face with Sue Masterson.

Mrs. Masterson did not reach out in love and offer pleasantries. Instead, she pointed out the front window and jabbed her finger as she enunciated each word. "Do you have any idea what your daughter is doing?"

She'd forgotten all about Heidi. Theia glanced about, expecting to find her daughter standing with some friend in the service. But Heidi wasn't in the sanctuary. Mrs. Taggart, her Sunday school teacher, had already come into the room and had situated herself with her family. Theia gave a half-guilty shrug. "Well, no. I guess I don't."

"You'd better go find out." Sue planted her hands on her hips and gave a righteous toss of her hair. "She's outside in the parking lot terrorizing little children with snowballs."

"Oh, that's ridiculous."

Theia knew this about herself. Above all else she would fight for the honor of her family. She'd done the exact thing when she'd gone to speak with Julie Stevens about Heidi's dancing. "I'll bet those kids are all having fun in the snow."

In her velvet skirt. In the forty-dollar clogs I

bought her from Broadway Toys-n-Togs.

"You ought to see what she's done to Dillon. He's drenched from head to toe. I'm embarrassed to bring him into the service. Water is running from his hair. He's out there *crying.*"

"He's crying? Because he got a little wet?"

"He's crying because your daughter shoveled snow down his pants."

Oh, dear. For the first time since her father had sung 'Purple People Eater,' Theia found something comical. She felt like doubled-over, stitches-in-her-side, bellyache laughter. Glorious. Splendid. But Sue Masterson had to go and spoil it all. "For heaven's sake, Theia. Your kids are the preacher's kids. They're supposed to act better than everyone else, aren't they?"

I can't do this, Lord. I cannot do this.

Without telling Joe where she was headed, she laid her Bible in the chair and ducked out. She hurried to the front vestibule to find her coat. There she found poor Dillon Masterson, his hair plastered flat to his head and a dark patch of wet spreading down to the knee of his cargo pants.

BELOVED.

A Savior's calling, in the midst of a mother's mile-a-minute day. Theia had come to the end of herself. But she kept going

72

anyway, not heeding the gentle summons in her spirit. She tilted her head at Dillon. "You okay?"

He nodded.

"So Heidi did this to you?"

He nodded again.

She rumpled his wet hair with her one operable arm. At least *some* good had come of his snowball fight. His face was cleaner than she'd seen it in weeks. "You go on in there with your mother."

"But I'm wet."

"The Lord doesn't care if you're wet. Only mothers care about something like that." She gave him a little pat-shove in the proper direction.

Theia found a troupe of fifth graders outside, acting like they owned the world, bellowing and running and smearing each other with snowballs. She got there just in time to see Heidi get walloped in the head.

Heidi wasted no time in retaliating. She scooped up snow, packed it hard between her hands, and let it fly. "Take *that,* you slimeball!"

The sphere hit its target, Trey Martin's backside, and exploded into icy particles. "Heidi Louise McKinnis!" Theia shouted. "You come here this instant!"

Amazing how silence could fall on a group

of fifth graders. "Hi, Mom."

"You want to tell me what's going on out here?"

"Snowball fights. We're killing each other."

"Do you think this is the proper place to be, out in the parking lot calling your classmates 'slimeball' while there's a worship service going on inside?"

"But it's *snowing.*"

"I know, and if I were ten years old, I'd feel the same way. But I'm not. I'm your mother. And Dillon Masterson is inside with a major problem."

"Am I in trouble?"

"That depends."

"On what?"

"Do you think you owe Dillon an apology?"

"No."

Theia stood in the snow, waiting, using the silent, stern approach, hoping her daughter would recant. But Heidi did no such thing.

"You won't apologize?"

"No."

"You'd better examine your heart, young lady."

"You should have heard what he said at school on Friday, Mom. He told Miss Vickers that the only reason I got moved up from angel to clown is because you've got cancer, and everybody found out, and they got worried if they didn't let me dance some other part this year that you'd never get to see it."

The force of Dillon's words almost knocked Theia to her knees. She felt like she'd been booted in the gut.

"I told him you were going to see me dance plenty. I told him he was stupid."

"Well, good for you. That's exactly what you needed to say."

"Dillon says I dance like a *chicken*."

"That is a cruel thing to say." The words pushed Theia to the brink. Her words blazed with passion. "*Listen* to me. You are a beautiful dancer. A *wonderful* dancer. You dance like a princess." Oh, how she wanted to say more. Oh, how she wanted to tell Heidi that she'd gotten the part because Julie Stevens must have noticed how she'd improved, or how she'd learned new steps, or how hard she'd tried. Theia cupped her daughter's cheeks inside her own two cold hands. "Do you hear me? Don't you ever let *anybody* tell you that you can't do something you want to do."

I can't do this, Father. I can't tell her Dillon's wrong about me. What if this is the last time I see Heidi dance?

Heidi grinned, her face innocent and open. "Mom, I know he isn't right. Don't you listen to Dillon, either. That's why I shoved snow down his pants."

"Let's go inside."

"I like it out here. Let's have another snowball fight."

"Your father will be disappointed if we miss his sermon." Mother wrapped one arm around daughter, and they sauntered hip to hip toward the door. "You know how he always likes us to tell him that it was good."

"Yeah, Mama. I know."

But Theia wondered, as they entered the front vestibule, whether she'd ever be able to know again that God and faith were good.

CHAPTER FIVE

Theia spent all Sunday afternoon digging in her cedar chest, looking for her hair ribbons.

They had to be here somewhere.

She found a pink plastic toy telephone, three of her own baby sleepers, and a tulip quilt that had been hand stitched by Joe's great-grandmother. She found a little purse made of white rabbit fur, a pair of gloves, and a box of silkworms someone had sent Edna from China.

But no hair ribbons.

If they weren't in the cedar chest, she didn't know where she might have put them. Maybe they had gotten put away with some of the girls' baby things. Maybe they were still attached to some ancient pair of shoes. Maybe she'd accidentally stuck them in the pocket of some old dress, something she'd dropped off at Browse and Buy.

Theia tried to remember when she had

last seen them. She poked her head further into the chest and kept digging.

"What are you looking for?" Kate flipped off the light to the bathroom and came out.

Theia spoke from beneath a pile of wool blankets. "Those hair ribbons I was telling you about."

"Here. I'll help."

"I'm almost to the bottom. I don't think they're here."

"What's this?" Kate held up one of the sleepers.

Theia glanced up and kept digging. "That was mine. Isn't it pretty?"

"Yes."

"I've saved your sleepers, too. I've got them put away in a box in the attic."

"I like it when you save things."

"Good. Be sure and tell your father that next time he's in the mood to clean out the garage." Theia pulled out her head and brushed off her hands. "I wish I could find those. I really wanted to get them out before I start chemotherapy tomorrow."

"I've got to go, Mom. I promised Jaycee I'd help her with her English project."

"That's okay."

"But I promised I would help you find them."

"I haven't seen those ribbons in years,

Kate." Theia said, her face flush with disappointment. "I'm afraid they're gone for good."

Joe and Theia lay side by side in the bed, Joe with his big study Bible propped open on his chest. Theia with the pillow plumped up beneath her neck as if she'd fallen asleep.

He knew from her breathing that she hadn't.

Joe turned a page in his Bible, looked at it, turned back. He had no idea what he'd just read. "You want me to go with you tomorrow?"

"Go with me where?"

"To chemo."

"There isn't any need for you to. They say I won't feel bad until I've had several sessions. The effects are cumulative."

"I'd still like to be there."

Theia readjusted the pillow beneath her head and snuggled down deeper. "I don't want you to come, Joe."

When she pushed him away like this, it made Joe feel more helpless than ever. "I want to support you, Theia. I want to be there for you."

"I was asleep. You woke me up."

"No, you weren't."

She sighed, but didn't disagree with him.

"Was the sermon okay today?"

"It was good."

"I'm not so sure."

"It was."

"Frank Martin looked bored. And Sue Masterson couldn't stop drying off Dillon with Kleenex the entire time."

"Hmm."

She answered with brusque, short sentences, his cue that she wanted him to be quiet. He shut the Bible with a crack and laid it on his bedside table. Then he waited, watching, hoping his wife would turn to him, only she didn't.

"Theodore?"

"Hmm?"

"How long do we have to wait before . . ." He couldn't figure out exactly how to say it. "Well, you know."

He heard her voice catch. "We don't have to wait if we don't want to."

But she didn't move toward him. She didn't move at all.

"Or we can."

"Yes."

A good five minutes of silence passed between them.

Outside the parsonage a hay truck rattled past, carrying its two-ton limit, on its way to deliver a load to one of the local ranches.

The lampshade rattled. They could feel the truck's wheels rumbling up through the floor. Joe stared at the ceiling above them; Theia stared at the wall on her side of the bed.

He thought of what he would do, loving her the way he did, if he ever had to go through one day without her.

She thought of what it might feel like to be gone from this earth, to be looking down upon them from heaven. She wondered what would happen to the girls if she died, and who would take care of Joe. So much she'd miss. All their silly jokes. Sewing those maddening patches onto Heidi's Girl Scout vest.

Sorting Joe's socks.

The weight of everything they carried together tonight felt like the truck outside with its huge load of hay, running across their hearts, crushing them both.

"Theia." This time, Joe couldn't keep himself from reaching out to her. He turned back the covers and placed his hand in the crook of her shoulder, bunching her night-gown in a way that had always given him pleasure. Beneath the cool sheer of the fabric, she felt the way a wife should feel to her husband; warm, compliant, soft, every-thing he needed. The slightest bit of pressure now, and she would roll toward him, loop her arms around his neck.

"My b-b-breasts aren't there anymore," she sobbed up at him as she wrapped her forearms around the nape of his neck. "You sh-shouldn't expect me to be b-b-beautiful anymore. I'm all c-cut away."

He wanted so badly to reassure her, but his words rang hollow in his own ears. "That doesn't matter to me."

"It does matter. You'll have to help me change the dressing soon, and then you'll see it. It's awful."

"But you are still *you* inside. You'll still be beautiful, Theia."

"My body looks like someone tried to sew up the corners of a cushion."

"None of that makes any difference to me."

"It *will*. I hate cancer. It isn't fair."

"You know what makes you beautiful to me? I've watched you give birth to my babies. That's what makes you beautiful."

"Why would God make this happen to me when He also made it happen to my *mother?*"

He didn't know why he made the next mistake. He'd stopped thinking perhaps. He was enjoying winning her over, saying all the right things. "I know how goofy you acted when we were young. That's what makes you beautiful to me. Because I was with you the time you stood up on the roller coaster at Lagoon. That makes you beautiful. Because I know you're going to be all snaggletoothed and funny-looking when we both get old together. That's what makes you —"

It took Joe a full ten seconds to realize the horrible, wrong thing he'd said. He froze. For a moment she just lay there, staring up at him like she hadn't heard him right. As realization hit, her countenance crumpled. Her chin began to quiver. Her mouth contorted. Her eyes welled with tears.

"Theodore, I'm sorry. I'm so sorry."

She shoved him off, cast the rest of the blankets aside, and jumped out of bed. "How could you say that? *How could you talk about growing old?*"

"I didn't mean to. I wasn't thinking. I'm sorry."

She pulled on a sweatshirt over her night-gown. She stepped into her snow boots and shoved her arms into her coat.

"Where are you going?"

"I don't know. I'm just *going.*"

He was up and beside her. "I'm coming, too."

"No, you aren't. I want to be alone."

"It's the middle of the night. You can't go out there by yourself. It's cold."

She screamed the words at him. "I'm a big girl, Joe. I go out walking, at all times of day and night, *by myself.* Just because you've said something stupid doesn't give you the right to come along with me!"

He couldn't stop himself. He'd borne his own burdens too long. "How can you act like this is just about you? If something happens to you, Theia, it happens to both of us. If you die —" He stood in the middle of the room, amid blankets that had fallen to the floor in angry knots, his hands balled into incapable fists at his side. "If you die, everything for me ends, too. You have to think about us together, not just you."

Theia walked away and didn't look back. She shut the door soundly behind her. Joe sank to the side of the bed, feeling totally cut off from his wife, wondering what had happened to the woman he'd been able to share everything with. "Please, God," he whispered aloud. "Please, God."

But that was as far as he could go. When he tried to find words to speak his heart, he found he wasn't able.

Theia's hurt hammered with every beat of her heart, a rhythmic throb of grief. She pulled her coat tighter as she stumbled across the unbroken snow, her boots stamping waffle patterns behind her.

When she looked over her shoulder, she could just make out the shape of the church and the parsonage and her dad's greenhouse, pink-washed in the moonlight. Theia stared up at stars, pinpricks in the night sky. She listened, heard only unerring silence, only the rustle of breeze in the trees. She stood in the midst of the snowfield, her lanky shadow lengthening in the moonlight, her own steps solitary behind her, and cried. "I c-can't do this. I can't be strong for everybody else. I can't even be strong for m-me."

So many things she needed . . . to be held close and rocked, to hear the affirmations that everyone around her could no longer give. To hold her children close and know that she would be alive to enjoy their growing.

"You've got so much food here," Laura Jones had said last week when she'd brought over lasagna. "You aren't going to have to cook for a *year.*"

She cried because Joe said she'd be beautiful when she was old. She cried because Laura Jones had taken stock of her refrigerator.

You won't have to cook for a year.

Did it occur to anybody that she might *want* to cook? That she might hold dear a hundred different chores because nothing guaranteed that she'd be around for those chores in another year.

I didn't want Joe to see me, to touch me. And maybe that's one less time for him to touch me in the time that we have left.

"Nobody understands, Lord! Nobody understands."

How she yearned for her father's arms. Not the feeble, aged way he held her lately, but the strong, big way he'd hugged her when she'd been a little girl. When he'd lifted her to the mirror so she could match her face to his. When he'd picked her up and carried her upstairs to sing "Purple People Eater." "I c-can't do this." Her nose ran, and tears rolled down her jaw to soak the collar of her coat. She did nothing to stop them. "I'm *mad* at You! Mad. How could You *do* this?"

She'd never been so afraid in all her life.

She'd never been so *angry.*

"Why would I have to drag my own two children through this?"

Clearly, as clearly as if a friend touched her on the shoulder and said, "Look and see," Theia saw her eighth birthday. A truck

86

from Preston Lumber had turned into the alley, with a crane on it so big she thought it might knock the neighbor's fence down. The crane lifted her new playhouse, its wood fragrant and stark, into the corner beside the patio.

Her daddy hugged her.

Her mama carried out boxes of doll furniture.

"Here are curtains." Her mother handed her a box. "You want to hang them up?"

"She's going to have to wait fifteen minutes or so, Edna." Harry waggled a screwdriver in the air. "I don't have the curtain rods hung yet."

She ran from one window to the other and peered in. "Can I bring my dolls out here, Mama?"

"Of course you can. That's what it's for. A place they can live." Her mother held out something flat in her palm. "Here's something else."

There in her hand lay a doll-sized embroidery framed in a hoop, carefully signed and dated: *Jesus Loves Me, This I Know.* Mama kissed Theia on the forehead. "Now it will feel like home."

That had been a long, long time ago.

No dolls anymore, but real daughters.

No tiny wooden furniture, but a living

room of Thomasville instead.

Jesus Loves Me. . . .

Do You? Do You really? Because if You do, why would You take Mama away? Why would You let it happen to her, and then to me, too?

The childhood images faded away, replaced by cold, stone reality. Dr. Sugden, aligning the charts and the diagram flat on his desk for her to see. Class IIA cancer. Upper right quadrant of the right breast.

"Not the sort of cancer that goes away without a fight," he said. "The sort that, if you live, you live with. The sort of cancer that if you survive it makes you certain that you are a survivor."

Where are You in this, Father? I can't find You, no matter how hard I try.

If He loved you, if He cared about you, none of this would have happened. A God who loves His children wouldn't let anything like this come into your life.

I HAVE DRAWN YOU WITH LOVING-KINDNESS. I HAVE LOVED YOU WITH AN EVERLASTING LOVE.

That means He isn't there at all, don't you see? If He were there, you wouldn't feel like He wasn't. You wouldn't have this awful emptiness inside. He'd be beside you, every step of the way. It's easy to tell that He isn't.

WHO SHALL SEPARATE YOU FROM

THE LOVE OF CHRIST? SHALL TROUBLE OR HARDSHIP OR PERSECUTION . . . ?

Fool. How could you believe such a ridiculous thing after what happened to your mother?

The lurid, dreadful voice in her head drowned out every other sound, every other thought, as she stood alone in the snow.

Her cheeks were wet from crying. She turned back toward the house and toward the bedroom where her husband would keep his back toward her, pretending to sleep. Her breath came as mere wisps of frost.

And her heart broke in the icy darkness.

Chapter Six

Harry Harkin lay wide-awake in his bed for the third night in a row.

Why can't I stop thinking, Lord? Why won't my mind shut down for a while?

He couldn't look at his daughter, at all those gauze bandages he knew were wrapped around her chest and her heart like armor, without thinking of Edna, of Edna's bandages, Edna's faith.

Harry didn't have to reach for the clock. When he woke up like this, he always knew the time: 3 a.m. Right on the money.

Last night when he'd been jolted out of sleep, he'd been stupid enough to punch the button. The clock spoke aloud, a woman's tinny, electronic voice from this clock he'd bought at K-Mart because he was getting old and he couldn't see in the dark without finding his spectacles.

"The time is three-oh-three a.m."

This morning, he didn't ask the confounded thing again.

He knew.

For six weeks after Edna died, Harry wouldn't touch her things. He'd left her belongings right where she'd arranged them, small cherished altars that kept him feeling close to his wife even after she'd gone. The small blue jar of Vick's VapoRub on her nightstand. A basket of Betsy McCall paper dolls. The crumpled hanky that still smelled of Emeraude. Her favorite pearl earbobs. As if she'd come back for them tomorrow, poke them in her pocketbook, laugh at him for thinking she might not need them anymore.

Then had come the day when he couldn't bear her things sitting around any longer. He'd swept through the house like a drill sergeant, his anger so tangible and hard that he'd taken no prisoners. *Sweep,* into the box everything went. Family photos that she'd loved. Notes from the children. The grocery list he'd kept like a shrine on the counter, the last one she had scribbled in her own hand: "Don't forget laundry detergent, ground beef, toilet paper."

Gone.

The Vicks and the bottle of Emeraude. Purses and hankies and even her favorite red polka-dot apron.

Gone.

He scrounged through the laundry room shelves, searching for packing tape. When he couldn't find anything better, he sealed the box shut with black electrical tape instead. He wanted this sealed. Finished.

Over and done with.

Lord, why the urge to see what's inside the box now? Why, after all these years?

He'd endured. He'd made precarious peace with his heavenly Father, if only to bring himself to a place of somewhat baffled acceptance of Edna's death.

Wouldn't digging through Edna's personal effects open wounds again, Father? Can't I keep those old hurts sealed in the recesses of my heart? I know myself. If I let myself relive that now, I stand to lose the hope I still have for my daughter.

He reached toward the nightstand and thumped the button on the clock.

"The time is three-oh-two a.m."

A shadow flitted past his window. Harry sat up and fumbled for his bifocals. He saw Theia trudging through the snow toward the parsonage. He watched as she back-handed her nose with a mitten. She'd been crying.

The time is now, his heart pulsed to him in

92

its underlying, faultless rhythm. *The time is now.*

None of us can go on like this, Father. What is it that You want me to do?

That afternoon so long ago, he'd backed the Fairlane out of the garage, propped up the ladder, and stowed Edna's things as far back as he could get them into the corner. He'd moved that box with him three times. After all these years, he'd neither unfastened it nor looked inside.

No sense in mistaking an old man's folly for the Spirit of the Lord.

He asked the question aloud in the darkness, his forehead still pressed up against the cold windowpane. "You want me to open all that up again, Lord? Sure don't see what good it'll do anybody."

Silence.

No reassuring voice in the darkness.

Only the dull aching of his heart, the memory of the day when he'd swept through room after room, fighting to purge every painful recollection, every broken promise, from his household and his life with his little girl.

Theia decided the hair ribbons had to be in the buffet.

Digging for hair ribbons seemed as good

a therapy as any after her sleepless angry night.

She wasn't due at St. John's for her chemo treatment for several hours. She had the entire morning to herself. She got down on her hands and knees and, piece by piece, began to bring out the tiers of plates that made up her wedding china. First came the Gorham Rondelle saucers, then the dessert plates, then the bread and butters. Even though she was a preacher's wife, she was a preacher's wife in Wyoming. She hadn't set a table with these fancy dishes in ages.

Just to make sure, she checked the stacks of linen napkins and the basket she used when she served dinner rolls. She checked inside the plastic sack where she kept Christmas candles, wrapped in tissue.

She sat back on her heels.

There wasn't anything here.

"You know what I wish for?" she said aloud to nobody there. "Maybe some pictures. Something to put around the house that would remind me of . . . *me*."

Even as she said her wish aloud, she realized how she could make it happen.

Beneath the maple lamp stand in the front room sat a row of thick photo albums, dating back to the days when the girls had worn diapers.

Theia piled the Gorham back into the buffet and then sat cross-legged on the floor beside the lamp stand. She unshelved each album and thumbed through it, occasionally slipping a picture out from behind the plastic, reading the back, checking its date. Some she put back where they belonged. Others she kept on the floor beside her.

An hour passed, and she'd only gotten halfway through the albums. An array of photos lay strewn in a circle from her right ankle to her left knee.

A snapshot of Joe holding a large Mackinaw trout.

A backside view of Kate as she stood, topless and toddling, trying to reach a watermelon bigger than she was in the refrigerator.

A black-and-white picture of Theia's best friend, Bobbie Galden, riding a horse.

The girls with their Easter baskets, squinting into the sun.

Then, her favorite, one she'd kept forever and hadn't looked at for years: the litter of kittens she hadn't wanted to part with when she'd been ten. In this photo, she wore her two blue hair ribbons, tied at jaunty angles, one on each pigtail.

She would just have to be satisfied with a picture.

She couldn't come up with those hair ribbons any other way.

If Theia hurried, she had just enough time to take these to Big Horn Photo on the way to St. John's. She would buy pretty frames at Global Exchange and arrange them according to size on the table behind the sofa. She would display a few on the mantel. She would scatter some beside lamps and along windowsills.

Forget the expensive decorate prints and the watercolor she and Joe had bought each other for their tenth wedding anniversary and the pencil etching of a moose by the pond that they'd won top bid in a church auction.

Unnecessary adornments would come down from her walls. She would fill this house with life. Her life.

Joe fanned out the pages of his sermon across his desk and tried to make sense of them. He scrubbed his eyes with his palms, picked up his pen and made a note. Then he stared at what he'd written for a full fifteen seconds before he shook his head, drew a line through the entire thing, and pitched the pen across his desk.

The backbone of his Sunday message. Gibberish. He'd worked on this for hours, and now it made no sense at all.

I'm a failure at being a husband for her, Lord. I don't know what to say to give her strength. I don't know what to say to let her know how much I love her. Even when I do think I know what to say, I open my mouth and the wrong words come out.

Stupid words. Hurtful words.

WHAT GOOD ARE YOU, HUSBAND, IF YOU HAVE FORGOTTEN TO RELY ON THE ONE WHO SEEKS YOU FOR HIS BRIDE?

Joe picked up the pages of his sermon one by one, scanned them, crumpled them into wads, and flung them against the wall.

Who am I to think I can teach anybody about You? Who am I, that I've taken responsibility for shepherding Your flock?

Joe stood in the middle of the office where he'd counseled close to hundreds, waiting, his breath coming in short laborious wheezes, his own heart an empty cavern.

He raised his fist to the ceiling and shook it. "Show me, Father. Show me who I am!"

The room felt as empty, as cavernous, as the portions of his own self that he'd finally opened up and laid out upon the winds of the heavens. Joe knew this to be true: Nothing about him was worthy or good enough or strong enough for the task that had been laid before him.

Joe lowered his arm.

He closed his eyes.

When he did, the picture came. Not so much a picture, maybe, but a living depiction. Moving figures. Wailing women gathering frightened children and herding them away. A trail of dirty, jeering Roman soldiers as they followed a bent man heaving a cross along through the dust up the hill of Golgotha.

Behind the cross stumbled this Jesus, this man they called the Christ, and Joe, standing alone in his office, saw the human man as he'd never been able to see Him before.

Their voices shrieked at Him as He staggered onward up the hill.

"Hail, king of the Jews!"

Again and again they struck Him on the head with a staff. One of them ran ahead, fell on his knees, paid mocking homage to Jesus as He passed.

"Hail, king of the Jews! Oh, mighty savior of the world. If You could only save Yourself now!"

Spittle coursed down His face from where they spat on Him.

Joe watched, horrified, as the soldiers lifted the cross from the shoulders of another man and began to erect it. This, then, was as far as he needed to see. But even though Joe's eyes were closed, the scene remained.

He knew what would come next.

They would put thorns on Jesus' head that would dig into His scalp and rip out His hair.

They would pluck the beard from His chin until there was scarcely anything left of His face.

With a cat-o'-nine-tails, they would scourge Him until his innards hung out of His body and His skin was shredded into tatters.

They would pierce what was left of Him with a spear, and His blood would begin to pour out onto the ground.

His followers would desert Him. His friends would betray Him. Even His own Father God would have to turn away from Him.

"No," Joe whispered. "No."

They kicked Jesus and put a bag over His head and shouted taunts. And when the bag was ripped off, this human man turned and fixed His eyes on Joe with an expression that took Joe's breath away.

THIS IS WHO YOU ARE, JOE MCKIN-NIS.

This then, he saw, was love. Love with no

ulterior motive, unadulterated and true. The very definition of love, not in a dictionary, but on the cross.

"Lord!" Joe cried out as this man Jesus climbed past him, onward, to His crucifixion. "Lord!"

COME UNTO ME.

This is how God showed His love among us: He sent His one and only Son into the world that we might live through Him. This love: not that we loved God, but that He loved us and sent His Son as an atoning sacrifice for our sins.

At that moment, the room filled with a quiet gentle presence, a peace that vibrated to the very core of the pastor's soul.

"Lord?"

It had been so long.

So long.

COME THAT I MIGHT BEAR ALL YOUR BURDENS. COME THAT I MIGHT SHEPHERD YOUR FLOCK, EVEN AS YOU AGREED TO SHEPHERD MINE.

Joe fell to his knees, his kneecaps making a huge, hollow thud on the floor. He didn't care. His entire body shook. The trembling wouldn't stop, and he didn't want it to. He bowed before his Holy God, his tears pouring forth from the very headwaters of his soul. "I'm s-s-sorry. Oh, Lord, I'm so sorry. Oh, I'm sorry." He cried out like an orphaned child. "I've tried so hard to do the r-right things. And I've b-b-been so wrong."

He cried out the same way that the apostle Paul had cried out after he'd served thirty years in the ministry. "I want to know You, Lord. I've been looking at myself, not at You. Help me to stop imitating You, Lord." He lifted his eyes to the heavens. "I'm so t-tired of trying to live that way. All I want is to seek You, Father. You working through me, not me trying to do the right things anymore."

Help me with Theia, Father. I don't even know where to start. She's shutting me out.

And then, he knew.

Oh, Lord. I'm sorry for being afraid. I'm sorry for being selfish. I'm sorry for counting the cost for myself when I ought to have been thinking of her instead. Oh, Father.

A knock came at his door.

Joe stumbled to his feet. He didn't take the time to straighten his shirt, fix his hair, or attend to his face. He turned the knob and yanked the door open.

There stood Sarah Hodges, his secretary, with a cup of coffee strong enough to jump-start a Studebaker in her hands. She offered it to him. "I was just cleaning out the pot."

He'd thought she'd stare at him, only she didn't. Sarah was too busy taking stock of the wadded-up pages of sermon that had landed in various corners of the room. She finally met his eyes. Her brows furrowed. "You working on your Sunday message?"

"I am, oh, I *am*." He said it with such vigor, he splashed coffee dregs onto the carpet. It seemed years since he'd had this much joy, this much hope. He grinned and booted a wadded page of sermon out of his way. "Do we have any Coffee-mate for this, Sarah? It's going to make my hair stand on end."

CHAPTER SEVEN

Number nineteen, the regular Teton County middle-school bus, crept past the McKinnis's house at the exact same time every afternoon. Today, as the bus took the corner and made its way up Ten Sleep Drive, Kate had a minute to lean across Jaycee and scrub everyone's foggy breath off one window.

"See, you guys —" she pointed to the Fairlane where it sat waiting in the side yard "— I *told* you Grandpa was giving me his car. There it is."

"Whoopeee." Paul Jacobs pulled his Game Boy out of his backpack and started punching buttons. "That drools. What a piece of junk."

"It isn't junk. My grandpa's been driving it for twenty-seven years. He put a new battery in it and everything."

Paul won some sort of victory on the Game Boy, and it exploded into a mass crescendo of electronic sound. He rolled his eyes. "Like I said . . ."

"It rocks, Kate." Jaycee snuck her a red Twizzler, being especially careful because they weren't supposed to share anything to eat on the bus. "Paul is just jealous."

"It's a Ford."

"*F-O-R-D* stands for Found on Road Dead."

"When I get my permit, he said he'll take me out to the elk refuge so I can practice."

"I'll bet that car hasn't gone anywhere in ten years. It's buried in snow up past its hubcaps."

"That's because it just snowed this weekend, stupid. He drove it to the hospital last week."

The school bus hissed to a halt, the red stop sign folded out like an oar, and the huge yellow door accordioned open. "Stupid," Paul mimicked as Kate zipped up her Columbia jacket.

Jaycee waved. "See you later."

"Come over if you aren't doing anything."

"I will."

Kate hadn't thought to actually dig the car out of the snow until she saw the snow shovel propped beside the shed. *Hm-mmm.* If she cleared off the hood, her friends could see it better. Then annoying people on the

104

bus couldn't make any more comments about the Fairlane not going anywhere for ten years. "Mom! I'm home." She left her backpack on the floor where she wasn't supposed to leave it, and went to the pantry to find a snack.

Her mother had left a note on the kitchen counter. "Gone to doctor's. There all afternoon. Heidi @ dancing after that. Love, Mom."

Oh yeah. It was Tuesday. The day of her mother's first chemo session. Kate jammed her mouth full of Doritos, found the broom, and hurried outside to begin laboring.

First, Kate used the broom to sweep snow from the Fairlane's windows. Next she pushed snow off the car's roof. After that she brushed snow from each fender.

She stepped back to survey her work.

She'd left huge piles behind the wheels and in front of the headlights. This was going to be a lot harder than it looked.

Kate yanked the shovel out of the snow and started digging. She hadn't scooped more than a dozen shovelsful before her back began to ache and her thumbs began to throb. She kept shoveling anyway, slicing into the ice with the shovel blade, pitching the load off to one side until she had the beginnings of a path.

Just let Paul Jacobs try to say this car won't go anywhere!

Slice. Pitch. Slice. Pitch.

I could get in and turn it on and drive all the way to Colorado if I wanted to!

That thought kept her going a long time. She had no idea how long she'd been digging when Jaycee came walking up the street toward her house. "Oh my gosh. Kate! You're really digging out the car. Is your grandfather going to let you drive it somewhere?"

"Sure." Kate hesitated. "Sure he will. He might even let me take it on the highway if I'm careful."

"No way!"

She didn't know why it seemed important to one-up Jaycee, but just now, it did. "He said he would," she lied. "That's why I'm doing all this." Kate jabbed the shovel hard into the snow so it stood unaided in the middle of the path.

"You're so lucky."

Kate dusted the snow off her mittens, satisfied.

Jaycee pulled her stocking cap down further over her ears in frustration. "It's so boring riding bikes when everybody else is getting cars."

"It's your turn to spend the night here

Friday night. You want to?"

A long moment passed. Jaycee didn't answer right away. She slumped against the fender of the Fairlane and stared off into oblivion, looking guilty about something. At last she said, "I don't think I can."

"Why not?"

"You know." She shrugged easily, but Kate could tell something wasn't right. "There's always a whole lot going on."

"There's nothing going on. I'll ask Mom. She'll say it's fine. You'll see."

"I can't come over, Kate. Don't bother her about it."

Kate grew silent as she stored the shovel back in the shed, and the two girls walked together back toward the house. Suspicion niggled at her heart. Jaycee had never turned down a sleepover before. She asked with great caution, "You want to come inside?"

"That sounds good."

It was the right time of day to play music; her father was still working in his office at church. Kate grabbed the Doritos bag and the bean dip from the fridge.

"Paul Jacobs was being a total jerk today on the bus." Jaycee followed Kate upstairs. She paused, and then spoke the next few words with entirely too much emphasis.

"There are a lot of people being jerks right now."

"Including you."

"I can't help it."

Kate shrugged, trying to push the pain away, but she couldn't do it. "Did you take notes on Miss Rainey's class today? On 'To Build a Fire'?" They'd been reading a Jack London story in English. "Tiffany kept passing me notes, and I never wrote anything down."

"I wrote down some stuff."

"If you came over Friday night, we could study for the test."

"Kate, I've already said I can't come."

"Whatever." Kate's lips contracted into a tight line of hurt. "Sorry I asked."

Jaycee turned away and fiddled with the row of first place blue ribbons that Kate had mounted on her bulletin board with pushpins. She'd won them all at the Teton County Fair, entering art projects. Jaycee sniffed and her shoulders heaved. It took Kate about five seconds to figure out that her best friend was trying not to cry.

"You want to tell me what's going on?"

Jaycee shook her head, still toying with the ribbons. "I promised that I wouldn't. It stinks."

Kate thought of her grandfather's car

again, the Fairlane, out sitting in the snow, ready to cruise. Whenever things got bad, she thought of the car, and it made her feel better. But even that didn't help much now. "Fine then. I wouldn't want you to break any promises."

"I told you that everybody was being a jerk. Well, that means more than Paul Jacobs."

"Who does it mean?"

Jaycee turned around, drew a line with a finger beneath each eye to clear away tears without smudging mascara. "Tiffany Haas. She's having her birthday party Friday night, and she isn't inviting you."

Kate looked stunned. "She isn't? We're good friends. I had her to my birthday this year."

"I know."

"She kept passing me all those notes in Miss Rainey's class today."

"She's invited six people, and she's made us all promise that you don't find out."

It devastated Kate, everyone knowing the secret but her, being left out and alone. Her fair skin turned an angry red. "How come she doesn't want me?"

Jaycee didn't answer the question. "We're driving to Riverton. Her mother's gotten us a room at the Holiday Inn, and we're going to spend the night and swim. We're going shopping at the mall the next day."

Kate asked the same question again. "How come she doesn't want me?"

"If you ask her to her face, she'll have an excuse."

"Which is — ?"

"That there isn't room in her mom's Suburban for anybody else."

Kate tried her best not to get upset. In her head, she listed the names of Tiffany's other friends, girls Kate liked and would have wanted to shop with. It would have been so much fun to be a part of the crowd. "Maybe that's a good-enough excuse."

"It's a fine excuse. Only it isn't why."

"It isn't?"

"It's because of your mother, Kate. Because she has cancer. Tiffany didn't invite you because she was worried you might talk about your mother's cancer. Her mom agreed with her, too. She thought it wouldn't be fair, asking you to have fun when there was something so sad happening to your family. Tiffany's mother said she wouldn't know what to say."

To cry in front of your best friend is a disreputable thing. So Kate didn't cry in front of Jaycee now. The muscles of her throat moved in a convulsive swallow. Why did stupid people always worry about saying the right thing?

It wasn't fair. None of it.

Kate picked up the phone book and searched through it for Tiffany Haas's number.

Theia pushed herself up off the couch in the waiting area and watched Heidi through the one-way mirror in studio three. Heidi did her best to keep up with the other clowns, but it would take weeks for her to grasp this complicated dance. Even so, she bounded around the room to the strains of Tchaikovsky as if she'd been given a gift, springing forward in the circle and catching hands, grinning when she made a misstep, catching hands, trying it over.

At one point when she made a mistake, Heidi gestured with wild animation toward her teacher. The instructor nodded. Theia watched as everyone took hands again, circled once, broke the circle, and then whipped into it backwards. The teacher pursed her lips and tilted her chin, then began slowly nodding again. "That's great —" Theia could read her words through the glass "— Let's add it to the dance."

Theia stood in the hallway the way she'd stood so many times before, her hand barely resting on the temporary cotton prosthesis beneath her blouse. Somewhere deep in her belly, the queasiness and the exhaustion that the doctor had predicted had begun.

No one could tell her exactly how her body would respond to chemo or what to expect. Dr. Sugden had given her two IV drips, the first something supposed to quell nausea, and the second a liquid similar to red Kool-Aid that made her entire body hum like a guitar. They sent her home with a list of printed instructions. She was to call the nurse if she developed fever over 101, started bleeding or bruising, or if the nausea didn't go away.

Other people had been in the waiting room with friends, but Theia had brought no one.

Why couldn't I tell Joe that I was afraid?

The door had opened upstairs. Four or five little dancers came trampling down the wooden steps, their snow-booted feet clattering as they came. Inside the studio, the instructor started the clowns on their cartwheels. Even though Heidi couldn't hear, Theia whispered the same instructions her own mother had given her once, out in a grassy yard, somewhere long ago.

"Hand. Hand. Foot. Foot."

Come on, Heidi. You can do it.

"Hand. Hand. Foot. Foot."

Heidi moved across the floor like a gigantic broken turtle, shaking her head and laughing, trying to get her hands on the floor and her feet in the air.

At her side, Theia's fingers closed and then opened again.

I should have been able to teach her. I should have been able to take her out in the front yard and tumble across the grass with her.

At that moment, she felt like cancer had devastated her. Cancer had kept her from helping her daughter grow.

It certainly hadn't taken much time, calling the girls from Miss Rainey's class and having them all over. "I know about your birthday, Tiffany." Kate planted her hands on her hips and flipped her hair over her shoulder in defiance. "Next time your mother doesn't want me to come to something, you can just tell me. You don't have to talk to everybody in school first."

Tiffany tilted her head toward Jaycee. "You've got a big mouth, you know that."

"I can't help it. Kate's my best friend."

"I trusted you."

"If you didn't want me to tell Kate, you shouldn't have invited me in the first place."

113

Tiffany squared her hands on her hips, too. "Well, maybe I'm sorry that I did."

After all of the hurt and disappointment, Kate did her best to be the peacemaker. "It's okay, Tiffany. I made her tell me. I bugged her and bugged her until she'd say what was going on."

Jaycee didn't back off. "I'm going to stay here Friday night and spend the night with Kate."

"Fine. You do whatever you want to do. The rest of us are going where we can have fun. Nothing fun ever happens around this place."

Megan Spence, who had been flipping through CDs in the corner, gave out a little laugh. "Tiffany. This reeks. Of course there's fun stuff to do here. Kate has her own car."

"Yeah," Jaycee echoed.

"So what?" Tiffany was gathering up her things to go. "She can't drive it yet."

"Yeah. But *I* can."

All three girls stared at Megan.

She waved her billfold in the air. "I've got my hardship license right here."

Kate's heart froze.

"So." Tiffany slid her arms into her coat. "Why are we all sitting around here? Let's go somewhere."

"We can't do that."

"Why not? It's your car, isn't it?"

"Yes, but I haven't —"

"You've been bragging about it for days."

"I know, but it's not the way I've made it sound."

"Where can we go?"

"The library?"

"We can't make any noise at the library."

"I could get a book for my book report though."

"We could drive up and down Elk Refuge Road and listen to KMTN."

"We could go to Dairy Queen."

By the time they'd all chimed in, Kate could not say no. Only Jaycee glanced back at her with some hint of remorse as they went outside, glanced in every direction to make sure that nobody was watching them, and Megan started up the car.

"Where's your grandpa?" Jaycee asked as Megan backed out.

"I don't know."

Kate fingered the door handle. A piece of silver peeled off beneath her nail. The inside of the precious Fairlane smelled musty and old.

It wasn't supposed to be like this. It was supposed to be something special that Grandpa and I did together.

"Where's your dad?"

115

"In his office. He's got counseling appointments and stuff."

They stopped at the sign on the corner of Ten Sleep and made a right onto the highway. "Turn on the radio!"

"It's cold back here. Can you turn on the heater?"

"Just a minute! I have to figure out how to turn everything on." Megan turned on the radio, but it took a few seconds to warm up and start playing. "Kate, this car is really old."

"I know that."

They passed the turnoff to High School Road where the middle school and the high school sat side by side. They passed McDonald's, the Wyoming Inn, the pawnshop, and the Sagebrush Motel.

"I hate that song. Can you change it?"

"Where are we going?"

"Did anyone bring any money?"

They ended up at Dairy Queen. They pooled all their change and had enough to buy one Blizzard. They doubled back and drove halfway to Moose-Wilson Road. They honked at two different carloads of friends. They waved at the Teton County school bus bringing the Jackson Bronc JV football team home from a game. They hung a U-turn and started back toward the town square, heading for Elk Refuge Road.

That's when Megan glanced back over her shoulder at Kate and grinned. "It's your turn. You want to try?"

"Me?"

"It's your car, isn't it?"

Tiffany laughed nervously. "She can't drive, Megan. You're being crazy."

Jaycee sat beside Kate, her fists clenched at her sides, not saying a word.

Kate stared at her friend, her pulse drumming in her throat. She squirmed in her seat. They were all looking at her.

I can handle everything everybody's throwing at me. I can. "Well, it isn't a big deal." She said it mostly to Jaycee. "If Megan can do it, so can I."

"You can?"

"Sure."

Megan turned around again and eyed her from the front seat. "Kate, you're such a goody-goody. A preacher's kid. You know you don't really want to drive this thing."

"I do."

For what seemed an eternity, nobody moved. Tiffany finally flipped down the sun visor, opened her little pot of Carmex, and smeared some across her mouth. "It's not that big a deal. Everybody's tried it by now," she said with nonchalance. "Cheri Fraser walked home one day when her mom had gone to Dubois and drove us up to Yellowstone. We were gone all day."

"Driving ought to be easy," Jaycee said.

"You really want to try?" Megan's eyes met hers in the rearview mirror.

"Yes."

Kate had thought her positive answer would send them running from the car screaming, but it didn't. They sat right where they were, except for Megan, who pulled the car to the side of the road, got out, and gestured for Kate to scoot in behind the steering wheel. "Go ahead. I'll teach you."

Kate climbed out of the backseat, came around, and slid inside. She put her hands on the steering wheel. In her mind, the car grew ten times bigger. Kate leaned against the bench seat and felt the ancient upholstery crackle beneath her. She checked the rearview mirror, but all she could see were her own eyebrows, her own pale forehead.

"I don't think I want to do this."

"Just turn it on. Put the car in gear, and it'll go forward. That's all there is to it."

From where Kate sat, she could see Tiffany stretching her arm along the door beside the window, flicking her nails against the grid where the heat flowed.

Tiffany, who hadn't wanted Kate at her overnight party because having her might spoil the fun.

At this one moment, driving this car became a declaration of liberty for her, a way to show the whole world — God and her parents included — that she could handle growing up.

I don't need my mother! I can do things on my own.

Kate turned the key. The engine roared to life at first try.

It felt incredible sitting here, a powerful engine throbbing beneath the hood, as if Kate controlled the whole world.

"Put your foot on the brake first. Then you put it in drive."

Which one was drive? Kate manhandled the shift and moved the red line to *R*, which she decided must stand for "regular." They rolled backwards, bumping up over the curb.

"No. No! That's reverse," three girls hollered to her all at once. "Put it on the *D*. That's drive. That makes you go forward."

She pulled the stick down, felt a clunk beneath her.

"You're doing fine. Fine. Now press down on the accelerator. That other pedal down there."

"There's another pedal?" Almost as fast as she asked the question, she found it with her foot. The Fairlane lurched forward. Jaycee grabbed the door handle. Megan screamed.

Just try to take my mother away, God. Do what You want to do, but You can't scare me!

She thought she was laughing, but then she realized she was choking on her tears. Her chest heaved, expanding for the air it wasn't getting.

"You're driving in the bike lane."

She yanked the wheel and went too far, jerking the car left, across the yellow line into the turn lane.

"Put the car in park, Kate. Put it on the *P!*"

A pickup truck loomed in the turn lane, coming right at them. They all three screamed at her, "Move over! Kate!"

She craned her neck over her right shoulder to check the lane. A Suburban roared past. "I can't."

Brakes squealed. For precious seconds, Kate sought the brakes in the Fairlane and found only air.

Bumpers came together in a terrifying crunch of metal. The girls pitched forward. Gravel flew.

When the car stopped, Kate moved the

red line to *P.*

She ignored the tears of frustration and defeat as they coursed down her cheeks. Instead, she switched the key off like an expert and sat taller.

CHAPTER EIGHT

Harry had never been one for tearing up good boxes. He retrieved a table knife from the drawer in his little kitchenette, made one clean slice through the right end of the box, then the left. He cut across the center seam in the box, making a clean dissection. He laid the knife beside him on the carpet and steeled his heart against what he knew he would find inside.

He expected to throw open the panels of cardboard and have the scent, the very essence of Edna, come pouring out at him. But it didn't. Instead, when he bent back the lid, everything inside smelled bitter and brittle, decayed with age.

He recoiled.

How fresh and painful these treasures once had been. How old and lost they seemed to him now.

He sat high on his old haunches, allowing himself, for the briefest of moments, to feel cheated. For this he could blame no one but himself.

There could be no hurrying the grieving process.

Sealing this box had been his one desperate attempt to contain an unbearable, devastating hurt. A hurt that had proven impossible to escape. Harry had journeyed in its shadow for a lifetime.

Would that he had not locked away these memories, these precious belongings of the woman who'd slept beside him and held him and nursed him and encouraged him for thirty-one years.

Would that he had touched these and cherished them while they still bore the fresh scent of her, the recent grip of her hand, the rare allusion of her presence.

Harry edged close again and, with a sense of desperation, peered inside.

Lord, will You show me? What is it that You intend for me to find here?

With one tentative hand, he began to remove items from the box.

Edna's favorite polka-dot apron. A tiny bowl she'd kept on the kitchen windowsill where she laid her wedding rings when she took them off to wash the dishes. Her darning thimble, kept in the wooden sewing basket beside her feet, worn so thin where she'd used it that daylight shone through the tin. The monogrammed mint green towel he'd found in the bathroom the day of her funeral, right where she'd left it, folded and lopped over the side of the tub. He lifted it high, let it fall open, seeking Edna.

He found only dust.

Harry refolded the towel and laid it aside with her other things. He reached in again. Touched leather. And knew.

Edna had always loved the feel of this Bible. He'd watched her when it was new, balancing it in one hand and running a palm over it with her other, enjoying the limber weight of it, the gold foiled pages, the way, when she dropped it open, it fell right to a place in the middle of Psalms.

He held it in both hands and stared at it.

It's only her Bible, after all. This is no surprise. I've known it was here ever since I closed that box.

Harry couldn't put it down. He remembered how she read every page of this book as if it were a treasure, lifting the page from the bottom right-hand corner, turning it slowly, smoothing the center of the leatherbound volume with the flat of her hand.

Father, what do You want from this?

As if to answer him, the Bible plopped open.

When he glanced down, expecting Psalms, he found something more. A vaguely familiar onionskin envelope with pink rosebuds and scalloped edges, like lace . . .

What *was* this? Harry was afraid to touch.

Edna had such stationery once. He remembered her writing notes on it.

He picked up the envelope and turned it over. What he saw made chills run up his spine.

"To Theia," it read in Edna's bold, slanted script.

In his own mind, Harry began to play devil's advocate, thinking of all the reasons this letter might not be what it seemed. Perhaps it had already been opened. Perhaps it was something Theia had already read, something day-to-day and childlike, not significant at all.

Harry flipped the envelope over again and checked the flap.

Still sealed.

Harry's chest went tight with anticipation. He understood the full truth. Theia had not read this letter.

She might never have seen it, if not for his digging in the box.

Emotion clogged his nostrils, misted his

eyes. Harry closed the Bible, leaving the letter exactly as he'd found it so his daughter could discover the envelope the way he had discovered it, the way Edna had intended it to be discovered all along.

He laid his wife's Bible with great care on the floor beside him.

Then he rocked back on his heels and whispered words of praise and gratefulness up to the sky.

Theia had just slammed the car door, opened the hatch of the Taurus, and lugged groceries to the kitchen counter when Joe came crashing in through the garage door. "Theia, did you hear from Kate this afternoon? Did she leave you a note or anything?"

Theia moved several grocery bags and checked the kitchen table, where they always left notes for each other if need be. "Nope. Nothing here. Where is she, Joe? Is something wrong?"

"Yes. She's been in an accident. A car accident."

"Oh, Joe, is she hurt?"

"Apparently not. Who was she with? Why didn't she leave a note to tell you she was going somewhere?" Joe gestured toward the car. They climbed in, and Joe backed out of the driveway, bumping over the wedge of snow that the plow left every time it cleared the road.

Theia buckled her seat belt. "I have no idea. She's always so good about that."

"She was with some friend. Jaycee maybe? I don't know who else would have come over after school."

"Joe, I —" Theia leaned her head back against the seat. The nausea she'd been battling all afternoon came upon her full bore. Her stomach roiled. "Joe, I'm going to be sick."

He pulled over for her at the corner of Ten Sleep Drive, yanked the door open, leaned over her, and held her head while she gave in to the effects of chemotherapy. She retched onto the graveled shoulder, gasping for air. "We've got to get there."

"We're okay, Theia." This time, his words didn't sound empty at all. He meant them. "She's waited for us already. She can wait a little bit longer." Joe searched the car for something so she could wipe her face. He found a pack of wet wipes in the glove compartment.

When Theia sat up and leaned against the headrest, he folded one of them to make a cool compress. He pressed it against her forehead, her temple, her other temple.

"Thanks," she whispered, shooting him a weak smile. "That's been coming on all afternoon."

"Are you okay to go?"

She closed her eyes and nodded. "Yeah."

They drove another three blocks, his knuckles white knobs as he clenched the wheel. Then in one abrupt motion, he steered them off to the right again and pushed the emergency brake on.

She stared at him. "Joe? What are you doing?"

For a long moment, he stared at his hands. Then he turned to her, spoke aloud to her the things he had given over to his Holy Father earlier. "Theia, I'm so sorry for so many things."

When she spoke, he heard hurt edging into her voice. "I don't think this is exactly the time to be discussing this."

"Perhaps it isn't, but we must discuss it soon." He took her hands. "Right now, there's something else more important."

She lifted her eyes to his. "What is that?"

"We have to pray. Together."

He saw her jaw go tight, saw the line of her lips begin to stiffen and then to tremble.

"I know." He touched her face, touched all the pain that he knew she still carried. "I know," he whispered, as he took her hands in his. He pulled them to him, entwined his fingers with hers, held them there.

"I can't pray."

He didn't let her go. "You want to tell me about it?"

She shook her head. "He wouldn't want to listen to me."

"He would. He *does*."

"I don't think God cares about me, Joe. How could a God who cares about His children let cancer come into their lives?"

"I've seen it, Theia. I've felt it. He's made me to understand His love better than I've ever understood it before."

"I can't see it. I can't feel it."

"What He feels about His children having cancer, He took to the cross."

"If He dies on the cross, He died for my sins, Joe, not for my cancer."

"All I know is this, Theodore. On that cross, He rendered evil ineffective. He took it upon Himself, and then He crushed it. Disease, sin, bad things, they haven't ceased to exist, but their power over His children has been broken. Your cancer has not been abolished, but it has been overthrown."

Her fingers curled into the safety of his hand. She stared at them there, and he followed suit. His fingers covering hers, their fingers wrought together like sinews of rope.

At last she spoke. "I was so wrong not to let you come with me today."

"I'll come the next time. And the next and the next. I am your husband. I want to be there."

Her two words, only a slight whisper. "Thank you."

"Will you pray with me for Kate, Theia?"

She nodded, tears in her eyes. "Yes, I will."

For the first time since she'd been diagnosed with breast cancer, they bent heads side by side, rearranged their clasped hands. "Holy God," Joe whispered, speaking aloud while Theia joined her heart with his. "Protect our daughter, Father. Keep her from harm. We can't do it, Lord, but we know You can. Surround her with Your angels. And give us renewed wisdom. Help us to know what to say, where to turn, when we see her. Amen."

"Amen," Theia said, too.

And thus for the first time in many months, husband and wife, mother and father, prayed together as one voice.

CHAPTER NINE

The fluorescent bulb glared overhead, bathing the sergeant's metal desk in sterile, harsh light. Theia watched her daughter sit in a wooden chair in one corner, rocking even though the chair was stationary, her hands trapped between her knees.

"Sergeant Ray Howard," his nametag read.

"Which one of you —" Joe wrapped one arm around Theia and held her next to him "— is going to tell us what's going on?"

Kate stared at her knees.

Sergeant Howard flipped a felt tip pen and caught it midair. "That ought to be up to your daughter, Pastor McKinnis. It seems she has a few important details that she needs to pass along."

"And the details are — ?" Joe stared at their daughter.

The sergeant flipped his pen again. "We couldn't find any insurance information in the glove compartment, for one thing."

Theia spoke to her daughter in a gentle, urging voice, the same way a child might urge a kitten down out of a tree. Even as she did, she realized that she and Kate had not talked, really talked, for weeks. "Kate, will you tell us what happened?"

Joe addressed the officer behind the desk. "What do you mean, you couldn't find any insurance information in the glove compartment? *What* glove compartment?"

"The glove compartment of that antique contraption your daughter calls a car."

"Our insurance ought not to be responsible. Whoever was *driving* ought to be responsible. Whoever owns the *car* ought to be responsible."

Sergeant Howard gave an exasperated little chuff of breath, and as if to say *It's in your court now, girl,* he shrugged at Kate.

"I was driving, Dad." Kate said it so softly that they almost couldn't hear her.

Stunned silence filled the room. Then, "What? What were you driving?"

"Grandpa's car."

Neither Joe nor Theia had the wherewithal to figure out how they had not noticed that the old Fairlane was gone. It sat in plain sight at the side of the house, where anyone walking past could see it.

Theia closed her eyes. *I've distanced myself from my family, Lord. I've been so focused on having cancer that I'm living my life as if I've lost everything already.*

Joe raked one hand through his hair. "Grandpa Harkin was going to *teach* you, Kate. He wanted to use the experience to help you grow up and become a responsible person. How could you just throw such a gift away? From someone who loves you like that?"

She shook her head, and Theia's heart broke as the tears pooled in her daughter's eyes. "I don't know, Dad. I really don't."

"*Is* the car insured, Pastor McKinnis?"

"I don't know. I'll have to talk to my father-in-law about that."

Theia left Joe's side and sank to the floor beside Kate, laying a hand of reassurance on her daughter's flank. "He doesn't have insurance on that old car, honey," she said to Joe. She turned to the officer. "It isn't a roadworthy vehicle. He had it out once, about ten days ago. But he didn't insure it. I'm sure he planned to take care of it before he gave his granddaughter driving lessons."

Sergeant Howard scribbled a note on the report. Then another. "The registration isn't up to date either. We found that out when we ran the license plate number. It hasn't been renewed in the state of Wyoming since 1989."

"Where is the car right now?" Joe asked.

"We've got it out in the impound lot. We towed it in with damage to the left front fender. And here's a copy of the police report filed by the driver of the other vehicle." He yanked a copy out of the clipboard and handed it over.

Joe took the papers but didn't read them.

Sergeant Howard ran his forehead back and forth in the flat of his hand. "So let's go over the charges, shall we? First, driving an uninsured vehicle. Second, driving a vehicle with expired tags. Third, failure to signal a lane change. Fourth, driving without a license. Usually in cases like these, where the driver has borrowed a vehicle from a member of the family, the family elects not to press charges of vehicle theft. But, I —"

"She's our fourteen-year-old daughter, Officer Howard. I doubt very much that her grandfather will want to prosecute."

"I'll need to talk to Mr. Harkin about that, I'm afraid. Although he hasn't phoned us to report the car missing at present time."

"He doesn't even know it's missing. None of us knew."

"Maybe if you kept a closer eye on your

children, Pastor, these things wouldn't come as such a surprise."

Joe's anger exploded. "How *dare* you accuse me of not watching over my own daughter?" He rose from the chair and advanced on the officer's desk. "If you had any *clue* what this family's been facing, you'd keep your comments to yourself."

"Honey —" Theia reached out to him "— Joe." *Lord, I don't want to distance myself from my own life any longer. I don't want to be distant from my children, from my husband, from You.*

Sergeant Howard slapped the clipboard on his desk the same way a judge would clap down a gavel. "She'll be scheduled to appear in Juvenile District Court two weeks from today, in front of Judge Terry Rogers. You are welcome to hire a lawyer or let Kate plead her case on her own. It makes no difference really. The outcome is generally the same."

Theia waited outside Kate's bedroom, her hand on the doorknob, her forehead leaning against the wooden door. Faint pop music played inside her daughter's room.

At last she gave a timid knock, once, twice, not knowing if Kate would invite her to enter or not.

"Hm-m-mm?" came a sleepy voice.

"Kate? It's Mom."

"Come in."

Kate was curled up in her single bed, propped up by pillows, reading a paperback novel.

"How are you doing in here?"

"Okay." Kate flipped a page of her book and kept reading.

Theia shoved her arms inside the big pockets of her bathrobe, touched one toe of her slipper to the other. "I just came to say good night. To tuck you in if you wanted me to."

Another page turned. "You haven't tucked me in since I was eleven years old."

"I know that. I thought maybe it was time to start it again."

On Kate's stereo, the CD player made a whirring sound and a click before it started playing another song. "I don't want to talk about today, Mom."

"It's okay." Theia didn't move toward her daughter. She stood in the middle of the room, feeling stranded. "I don't think I want to talk about it either."

Outside, gauze clouds stretched thin across the stars, and the moon shone transparent against the sky as though someone had tried to erase it. Theia's sense of loss settled someplace deep inside her rib cage, growing hard and heavy and cold there.

"I need to apologize to you, Kate."

"No, you don't."

"I've been a pretty crummy mom for the past few weeks."

Kate laid the book upside down, the pages forming a tent on her belly. "You haven't been. You've been fine."

"Even though I've been in this house with you, I've been far away."

"I can understand it, really. You've had some pretty crummy things happening to you lately."

Theia moved toward her daughter and sat on the edge of the mattress. The mattress creaked as it bore her weight. "There's no reason that you and your sister and your father should have to live through crummy things right along with me."

"Yes, there is." Kate rustled around in all the pillows and blankets until she could sit straight up beside her mother. "We're your family."

Another minute of silence passed. Kate pitched her book on the floor and flopped back three layers of covers. She patted the bed beside her. "Would you get all the way in bed with me, the way you used to do, Mom? Back in the days when we used to read stories?"

Theia touched her daughter's cheek and swallowed so hugely that they both heard it. "I don't know if there's room for both of us anymore. I haven't done this since you were —"

"Eleven years old." Kate smiled.

"We're both bigger than we used to be."

"That doesn't make any difference."

Theia crawled into bed with her daughter, turned on her side so they fit together like spoons. The Creator had cut them from the same family cloth. Their hips fit. Their bellies and their backs curved like instruments at the same places. Their shoulder bones jutted at the same angle, shadow images like limbs of the same tree, one alongside the other.

Kate moved over to give her mother more room. Theia scrunched around until she got the comforter adjusted. The bed felt wonderful. At last she could give in to the weariness that sapped her strength.

"Knock-knock," Kate whispered into the darkness.

"Who's there?"

"Little old lady."

"Little old lady who?"

"That's funny. I didn't know you could yodel."

138

Theia shook her head at her daughter.

"Didn't you get it? Little old lady who."

"I got it."

"I have another one."

"I'm almost afraid to ask."

"What did Snow White say when she took her film in to be developed?"

Theia couldn't help herself. She started to giggle. "I don't know. What did Snow White say?"

"She said, 'Someday my *prints* will come.' Get it? My *prints*."

That was all it took; they both dissolved in laughter.

They laughed until it hurt, pressing their faces into the pillows to keep from waking everybody else. They laughed until they cried. When they finally flopped over backwards, their bellies sore and their hearts lighter than they'd been in weeks, Theia rested her fingers on top of Kate's head.

She experienced at that moment an almost excruciating sense of the beauty, the texture, of life. She combed through silky strands of Kate's hair, reveling in the blend of its colors together, chicory brown and golden, sheening like water. She smelled her daughter's fragrance, sweet and fresh, like field clover tossed by a breeze. Even the bed linens exploded onto her senses, the entwining of the cotton threads, crisp and soft at the same time, a gift.

She thought of Heidi dancing in the studio, skipping across wooden honey floors, laughing at her missteps, her hair tucked behind one ear, her body pirouetting with joyful abandon before the mirrors.

The girls were each so beautiful and young and talented and . . . and *blessed.*

The world and all of heaven awaited her daughters.

How dearly she loved the two of them. She loved them fiercely, completely, to a depth that proved unbearable.

I HAVE LOVED YOU WITH AN EVER-LASTING LOVE, THEIA. I HAVE DRAWN YOU WITH LOVING-KINDNESS.

Her entire body quickened. Here, in this quiet place, lying in bed with her daughter, she could hear without distraction or debate. No other voices plagued her. Only the gentle, quiet declaration that delved deep, winnowed her spirit to its very core.

BELOVED.

He came to her, an audible voice out of the stars and the darkness and the breeze outside the window. She rose up in response to the waves of warm certainty and love that enveloped her spirit.

Lord? Lord, is that You?

Her heart waited, poised for an answer. It didn't come in the form she'd expected. It came as the seed of something deep and new, a jewel of wisdom, embedded securely in her soul.

All at once she understood something about herself that she hadn't understood before. All at once she held in her hand a freeing truth.

In the midst of her struggle with cancer, she'd spent the last weeks methodically counting the cost in her life. The time had come now to take the same careful account of every blessing.

Theia wound a strand of Kate's hair around her pointer finger, unwound it, and rewound it again.

I'm afraid, Lord.

LET GO.

Father, it scares me to let go.

MY ARMS WILL CATCH YOU. MY ARMS WILL HOLD YOU. DON'T YOU KNOW?

I know, but I don't know. Sometimes it seems so hard to believe.

There are times when the most eloquent prayers to the Father are the ones that contain no words. Theia took a deep breath, reveling as the air rushed into her lungs.

Surely, she wasn't alone. None of this had to be faced alone. She didn't have to figure it out or understand it. She curled up in the bed beside Kate and gave herself up, gave up all the burdens of her heart, her shame, her terror, her anger, her faithlessness, to the heavenly Father who already knew her heart to its very center.

And as she did, she knew something else. She knew her Lord's love. She felt Him holding her. She grasped the knowledge for the thousandth time and for the first time. She tasted how wide and how long and how high and deep was His love for her. He loved her, cared for her, more than her husband or her own daughters. All those earthly blessings were only a reflection of the love that He wanted her to know from the depths and the heights of heaven.

The love for her that He had carried to the cross.

After a long while she whispered, "Kate, I'm so glad to be your mother."

Kate nestled even closer against her in the single bed. "I'm glad you're my mom, too." A long pause, and then, "I know why I drove Grandpa's car today. I drove it to show you how independent I could be. I drove it to show that no matter what happens with you, I can manage on my own."

"Your dad and I both know you're growing up." But this went much deeper than just recognizing that Kate was maturing, and Theia knew it. "I'm here for you, sweetie. You can talk about all this stuff with me."

"I get really scared, Mom, when I think that something might happen to you."

It was what Theia had expected all along. *Put the right words in my mouth, Father. Please. I don't know what to say to her about this.*

Magically, miraculously, the words began almost to speak themselves. "Growing up doesn't mean that you have to grow independent, Kate. God wants you to rely on Him, no matter what happens. He wants you to know that, no matter how difficult things become, you'll never have to manage on your own."

Goose bumps raised on Theia's arms. She had no idea where any of this was coming from. *It's what You want me to learn, too, isn't it, Father?*

"I want to do that, Mom. I want to trust that much in the Lord."

"Oh, Kate, so do I."

It's so hard to let go, Father. Show me how. Saying something and doing something are two such different things.

Again her heart waited, poised, listening. Again the Father answered Theia in a different way than she'd expected. In the midst of her asking to be shown, the heavenly Father was already showing her.

He was using her to teach the lesson to someone else.

CHAPTER TEN

It was Thanksgiving morning, and the living room at the McKinnis household had been transformed into a room for a family feast.

While overzealous, overdressed television stars gave viewers a blow-by-blow description of the floats in the Macy's Thanksgiving Day parade, Joe added both leaves to their huge country oak table. He found his wife in the kitchen in her bathrobe, wrestling with the turkey and getting it ready to go into the pan.

He kissed the back of her neck, almost liking the idea that he no longer had to move her mantle of hair to do so. Since her hair had fallen out, first in strands and then in clumps, Joe had fallen in love with new parts of his wife that he hadn't seen before, the hollow at the base of her skull that perfectly fit the shape of his thumb, the swan arch of her spine that made her seem so beautiful and strong. He loved the way she wore gypsy-colored scarves knotted to look like flowers on her head. He enjoyed noticing her vast array of earrings. And for Christmas, he had already decided to give her diamonds.

"Hey," she said. He could feel her smiling even though he couldn't see her expression. "You want to open the oven door for this bird?"

He'd forgotten until he saw Theia struggle with the heavy roaster that her pectoral muscle didn't work so well these days. "Here, let me get that. You're trying to do too much."

"No, I'm not. Everybody's helping."

Indeed, they were. The girls would be up in no time and clamoring to get started on the pumpkin cake. Everyone that they'd invited to share in this day had insisted on bringing something: cranberry salad, mashed potatoes and gravy, fresh green beans, sweet potato pie. Even though everyone had offered to help, Theia could not be persuaded to give up cooking the McKinnis family turkey.

"Theodore. Promise me you'll lie down today and rest if you need to."

"I promise." She pecked him on the nose. "Thank you for agreeing to let me do this crazy thing."

"Not many people give huge holiday parties while they're battling cancer."

"I know that. But I want to see everyone."

"It's going to be a wonderful Thanksgiving."

"More wonderful —" a jangle of earrings punctuated her joy "— because I realize how much we have to be thankful for."

Because so many had insisted on helping Theia with the food, she'd been left free to arrange her table as she pleased. She'd sent her mother's antique-lace tablecloth off to Blue Spruce cleaners to be pressed. This morning she unfolded it and arranged the lace just as she wanted across the dark grain of the wood. At each place she set an index card with goofy turkey and pilgrim stickers. On each card at each place she'd written a different Scripture.

"Therefore, since we are receiving a kingdom that cannot be shaken, let us be thankful, and so worship God acceptably with reverence and awe." (Hebrews 12:28)

"Give thanks to the LORD, call on His name; make known among the nations what He has done." (1 Chronicles 16:8)

147

"Enter His gates with thanksgiving and His courts with praise; give thanks to Him and praise His name. For the LORD is good and His love endures forever; His faithfulness continued through all generations." (Psalm 100:4–5)

She stepped back and inspected her handiwork. The goblets stood polished and gleaming, ready for iced tea. The candlesticks stood tall and proud, a Mr. and Mrs. Pilgrim bedecked in Early American finery, a gift from Joe's mother one November.

Theia came to her own chair, the seat closest to the kitchen where she could jump up and retrieve condiments and refills when necessary. She set the card beside her goblet and read her verse for the umpteenth, glorious time.

"Let your gentleness be evident to all. The LORD is near. Do not be anxious about anything, but in everything, by prayer and petition, with thanksgiving, present your requests to God. And the peace of God, which transcends all understanding, will guard your hearts and your minds in Christ Jesus." (Philippians 4:5–7)

On the television the parade ended and football began. Kate and Heidi stood at the kitchen counter, arguing over who got to lick cream cheese frosting off the beaters. The doorbell rang. Theia's father arrived carrying a huge basket of chrysanthemums to sit beside the hearth, an assortment of breads from The Bunnery, and a gift, wrapped the way he always swathed his packages, in ancient tissue paper tied with string.

Before Theia had the chance to ask him about it, Sarah Hodges drove up with her family. Next came Winston Taylor, who shook Joe's hand roundly and hugged both of the girls. Jaycee appeared at the door with her parents, Lois and Tom Maxwell, and her two little brothers. "Happy Thanksgiving!" Joe welcomed them and took their coats at the door.

"Oh, Theia. What a beautiful table. Look at the Bible verses."

"Everything's so pretty."

"We made the cake." Kate held up a beater just to prove it.

"And everything smells so good!"

Not one person walked through the door without bearing a dish of something wonderful. Cakes and pies and casseroles vied for position on the buffet, then overflowed onto the coffee table. The very sight of so much food, the aromas, the ingredients, the hearts and hands that had prepared the meal, set Theia's senses reeling. She'd been having a difficult time eating since chemotherapy started. Even when the nausea subsided, she battled with a metallic tang that stayed in her mouth for days. She lowered herself into a chair in the dining room, gripping the back of it for support.

Lord, help me to be open and aware today. In the midst of my thankfulness, help me to be vulnerable and real. That's what You want from me, and I know it.

Eleanor Taggart sat beside her and touched her knee. "What can I do for you today, Theia?"

On her lips were the words, "Nothing. Everything's taken care of." But Theia realized that wasn't what she was meant to say at all. She thought for a moment and came up with something. "When the timer buzzes, will you take the dressing out of the turkey for me? Before Joe carves."

"I can do that."

"Thanks, Eleanor. For the time being, just sit and talk while I get my bearings, okay? All this food . . . well, I could use a little conversation."

"Yes. I will." A light, gentle smile. "How have you been?"

Theia had begun to understand, during

these past weeks, that this was the way she needed to be talked to. She needed to be asked easy questions, questions that let her choose between answering, "I've been driving so many dance carpools that I feel like a taxi driver," and "I had a rough chemo session this week, and my eyebrows fell out."

She understood that she needed to choose, more often than not, to feel cared for when people bumbled conversations around her and said the wrong thing.

With each passing day, the Father was helping her to know her own self and to trust Him more.

She chose truthful words for Eleanor now. "This week has been a good one, but there've been bad ones, too. I've been scared, and I've been discouraged. And I've spent the past days rejoicing that, for however long it lasts, I'm so lucky to be Joe's wife and Kate and Heidi's mother."

"It's tough going sometimes, isn't it?"

"You see this pottery?" Theia reached for a casserole filled with sweet potatoes. "It had to be formed and fired, painted and refired, for it to turn out as beautiful and colorful and *useful* as it is now. There are days when I feel like that's where I am, Eleanor. In the fire, burning up. That's when I have to remind myself that I'm in the kiln, being handmade into some useful new vessel for the Lord."

Eleanor squeezed her hand. "Your friends are here for you, to help you walk through this. We may not do it right, but we want you to let us try."

"Thank you." Theia hugged her. "I need to let you do that. For so long I've tried not to let anybody know that I was afraid. And I've been so alone."

The buzzer on the stove went off. Joe came into the kitchen with a troop full of men who brandished knives and planned to carve the turkey.

"Now that's a scary sight, all those men in the kitchen with knives."

"Out, out, all of you!" Theia grinned at Eleanor, rose from the chair, and shooed the men out of the kitchen with her apron like she'd shoo a flock of geese. "Eleanor has to take care of the stuffing first. Then we'll call you."

"We can just cut into it, can't we? The stuffing will fall out."

"Women have a way that they like to do things, and that isn't it."

Between the two genders, the great crowd of people managed to get everything uncovered and cut to serve, ice in glasses, tea poured, dressing in a bowl with a silver serving spoon, and a mountain of turkey sliced to perfection. Everyone oohed and aahed when Joe set the huge platter of meat on the table before them.

Winston Taylor volunteered to eat one of the legs whole.

Jaycee's little brothers began to shout at top volume for the wishbone.

Theia joined hands with Eleanor on her right and Sarah on her left. From across the way, her husband winked at her and then mouthed, "I love you." They had prayed together and had decided on the order of things just this morning.

Joe began. "Before we thank the Lord for the meal, Theia has something she wants to say to everybody here."

Lord, even while I walk through the valley of death, shine Your light through me.

"We invited you all here because we love you. Because the Lord loves you, too, and He's put you in our lives now, at a time when we need you the most." Her voice faltered. "We have not been easy to stand beside these past few months, but you have done it anyway. On this day of all days, when we offer up thanksgiving to our Father, we want to tell you that we thank God for you."

Down the table, Jaycee's mother, Lois,

picked up the index card that had been propped beside her goblet. Jaycee had told her mother about the Lord and had invited her several times to come to church, but so far she hadn't. "Can I read this?" the woman asked, her voice almost as shaky as Theia's. "I don't read the Bible much, but I'd like to read it today."

Theia nodded. "Oh, Lois. Please do."

" 'Come, let us sing for joy to the LORD; let us shout aloud to the Rock of our salvation. Let us come before Him with thanksgiving and extol Him with music and song.' "

Lois's gentle, hope-filled voice encircled the table even as they all encircled it with their hands.

Joe prayed after that, and everyone started passing the feast.

Theia hadn't been able to get back into her own kitchen all afternoon.

Kate, Heidi, and Jaycee had made quick work of the dishes. Others had served coffee and wrapped up the leftovers and left plates out with goodies for everyone to nibble while they watched football. Theia had even taken a nap.

It wasn't until almost dusk, after everyone had gone home and she went in to make a pot of tea, that she found the package wrapped in ancient tissue paper and tied with twine.

"What's this?" she asked anyone within earshot.

"Something your dad brought over when he came this morning. I don't know."

She untied the string, tore open the paper.

When she recognized it, her hands started to tremble. She couldn't swallow past the lump in her throat.

"Joe, this is my mother's Bible."

"How can that be?"

"I don't know. Dad must have found it somewhere."

Theia set her teacup down in the precise center of the saucer. She lifted the huge, leather book from its wrappings, and the pages fell open. Pencil notes, gleaned from her mother's favorite sermons and studies, lined the margins. In almost every chapter, verses had been underlined and some of them even dated.

"All of her notes are here. All of the things she was learning when she —"

Joe came up behind her and captured her shoulders. "When she got cancer?"

Theia nodded. "And before."

Her hands drifted to the brittle yellowed pages, fingering them as if they were gold.

Out the window she could see the light in her father's greenhouse, his dark silhouette stooped over the gardener's bench.

"I've got to talk to him."

Joe nodded, and she saw in his eyes that he understood. Love for her husband, for all they were becoming together, over-whelmed her.

She rose and went to find the other man in her life who loved her above all else.

Her father glanced up when she knocked on the screen. "Anybody home?"

He raised a trowel in her direction and gestured for her to enter. "That was a fine meal today, Theia. A fine meal." The light from the bulb above him seemed to catch in his eyes and gleam there.

She went inside, taking a deep draught of the smells of her father, of old fabric and of loose, dark soil in the greenhouse, of potash and bone meal and nitrogen and of new warm things growing outdoors. She held up the Bible in her hands.

"I found it, Daddy. Thank you."

He drove the trowel deep into the dirt. "Thought you could put that to good use right about now."

"I thought her Bible had gotten thrown out with the rest of her things. It's been missing for years."

He told her the story of how he'd sealed it away in the box.

"The more I kept praying for you, Theia, the more I kept thinking about that box. I swept your mother's life away before I'd scarcely even given you the chance to grieve for her. It was the wrong thing to do."

Theia laid her head against the rough flannel of her father's work shirt. It became difficult, at the moment, to discern who was holding whom for comfort. Her own father seemed so much smaller, so much more feeble, than she'd ever noticed before. As if he were withering away somehow. As if she'd become the parent and he, the child. "It's okay. You didn't know."

"Should have learned a long time ago. When you push aside the bad things, you also push aside God's power to heal and reconstruct."

"Maybe that's what God's doing now. Giving us both a second chance to heal."

Now that he'd dug all the dirt out of the pot, her dad selected a begonia from a plastic flat, turned it upside down, and emptied the squared soil and root into his gnarled old hands. "There's more inside that Bible than you've found."

"What do you mean?"

"Just look."

She began to thumb through the pages.

"There's notes all in here. And a church bulletin from some service back in 1979."

"Keep going."

At first Theia didn't see the envelope. But the page fell open, and she recognized the scalloped edge, the tiny pink roses, the paper as thin as an autumn-cured leaf. She picked it up. "What's this?"

"Maybe you can tell me."

She flipped the envelope over and saw her name written there in her mother's strong, slanted script.

Theia ran her fingernail under the flap and with the greatest of care opened a letter from her mother that had been sealed away for twenty-two years.

Dearest Theia,

If you are reading this letter now, it means that I have gone home to be with the Father, and you are looking through my Bible.

It is the most difficult thing I have ever done, thinking of leaving you and your father behind. But leave you behind, I must. I have faith in God and I have faith in the two of you. I know that, after I leave, you and your father will make it just fine. But you're going to have to help him a little bit. He's going to be lonely for a while, until he gets used to being without me.

I remind you now, and someday you will know, that healing is more than what some people think it is. To be healed is to be made whole. And I have been made whole, even though my body is against me, because cancer has made me realize that Jesus is here with me, loving me, telling me about myself, holding my heart. This has been, because of that new discovery, a most glorious time.

You, my precious daughter, are the one who has prayed the most for me. As I go, I stand firm on the belief that God does not cause cancer in this world. We humans mess up all of the time, but God never fails. Prayer must be, in the end, as in everything else, the perfect act of trusting God. Isn't relinquishment of everything to God very much the same as acceptance that God is in everything?

You have grown up so fast. You haven't worn these ribbons in your hair in a long time. I found them on the shelf beside my hairbrush today and thought you might enjoy having them to remember our mornings by. Being your mama is the joy of my life. You are a beauty, dear heart, inside and out, and I am so proud of you.

Mama

Two blue satin hair ribbons fell out of the folds of the letter, making two perfect curls in the flat of Theia's hand.

Theia held the strands of blue satin ribbon high for her father to see. They represented so much to her. A childhood that she'd almost let herself lose because parts of it were painful to remember. A loving mother who had done her best to teach her to grow and walk in courage and in freedom, despite the obstacle of disease.

Her father hoisted his latest potted begonia high upon the shelf. "Anything in that letter that an old man might get to hear about?"

"Plenty." Theia laid her head in a careful place, against the broad of his back where he still seemed powerful and young, where she could feel the strength of his heart beating. "She had faith in us, Dad. She knew we'd be okay."

Her father's voice was choked with emotion. "A good woman, my Edna." He turned and gave his daughter a sad, wise smile. "Guess it's time I stopped thinking about her dying. Guess it's time I started thinking about her living instead."

"Yes."

"She lived for us, Theia. She lived for us, and she lived for her Lord. Just the way you're doing now with your husband and your little ones."

For a moment, Theia stared at the ribbons, winding them between her fingers the same way she had wound Kate's hair not so long ago. She reached behind her nape and, with no further ado, looped them around her neck. She tied them into a double bow at the base of her throat. There would be no more ponytails or plaits for a while, not until her hair grew back.

"I always felt so special wearing these. I went through the whole day reminding myself that Mom had put those ribbons in my hair."

The same way she'd learned to get through each day with cancer, reminding herself of God's presence in her life.

Her dad took another tin bucket off the shelf and drove a nail in the bottom with one easy *thwack*. He turned it right side up and started to place rocks inside. "Remember how your mother used to stuff her Thanksgiving turkeys? Remember how she used to stand it upside down in the sink and wiggle its legs and tell us it was doing the tango so it wouldn't go down the drain?"

Theia tucked her mother's letter back inside the Bible, ready to carry it inside. "Oh, Daddy." She kissed him on the sandpapery cheek. "How could I ever forget?"

Opening night of the *Nutcracker* performance, and pandemonium reigned backstage at The Pink Garter Theater.

"My wing is torn." One of the littlest angels tugged on Theia's sweater. "Can you sew it for me?"

"I can't find my leotard." A reindeer jingled her bell harness for attention.

"The Sugar Plum Fairy can't find her crown."

Theia stood there, a corral mom helping out backstage, trying to figure out how to clean the grape juice out of Jake Mason's jabot before he had to dance in the party scene, dabbing circles of Shangri-La Ruby lipstick on each reindeer's nose, and making certain that no one chewed gum when she lined up to take the stage.

Ten minutes before the show began, Julie Stevens came behind the curtain and crouched close to her dancers. They gathered around her as she gave them last minute encouragement and suggestions.

"We've got a full house out there tonight, so be sure to dance your best. Angels, when you make the arch with your scepters, remember to make a slow big motion, big enough to carry to the last row of the theater."

Eight angels nodded, their halos bobbing.

"Mice, when you throw the cannonballs, remember that they are heavy. *Heavy.* You are not throwing plastic balls around. You are battling, iron against iron."

One mouse flexed her forearm and proudly showed everyone some muscle.

"Reindeer. I don't care what else happens out there, do *not* get too far ahead of the sleigh."

"We won't," they all shrieked while jingling the bells on their harnesses one more time.

"Sh-h-hhh."

"This is it. What we've been working toward for months. I'm on my way to the sound booth."

The dance students cheered.

Just as Julie Stevens headed downstage, she and Heidi almost collided. "Have a good time out there tonight, Heidi. You've worked really hard, and I'm proud of you." Theia's gaze locked with Julie's over Heidi's head. "I'm glad you're here tonight, Mrs.

McKinnis."

Theia inclined her jaw. "I am, too." That's all that needed to be said.

In the theater the overture swelled, and on stage the spotlights faded from twilight to black. They came up again in lavish colors, blue, green, red, yellow, bathing the set, a Christmas tree, an English Victorian parlor decorated for a party, in radiant light. Partygoers, young and old alike, began dancing their way up the aisles toward the stage.

"Are you going out in the audience to see me dance?" Heidi whispered.

Theia nodded. "I wouldn't miss it. They said I could sneak out and sit on the stairs to watch."

"Where are Grandpa and Dad and Kate?"

Theia opened the side of the curtain just an inch. "Over there." She pointed. "See. On the fourth row."

There they sat, all three of them, already enthralled by the performance, their faces captured in the vivid lighting. Theia closed the curtain. Heidi nodded at the double bow that Theia had pinned to the chest of her sweater. "You wear those ribbons Grandma gave you all the time now, don't you?"

"Yes, I do. I brought them along for a

special reason tonight though. Just in case you thought you might want to borrow them."

Heidi checked her braids, pinned with what felt like six hundred bobby pins and sprayed with hair lacquer so they wouldn't give way during the cartwheels. "There isn't anyplace to put them."

"If you wanted, we could always come up with something."

"What if I mess up the cartwheels after I've practiced them so many times?"

"Remember what I taught you. It's all in the rhythm. Hand. Hand. Foot. Foot."

"Can you tie a ribbon on my arm, Mom? That way I'll know it's there, but no one else can see it."

"Ah. There you go. Perfect idea." She unpinned the ribbons from her sweater and made a lovely bow on her daughter's arm with a flourish. "I'll be praying that every cartwheel lands right."

Heidi pulled her sleeve down over the little bow.

"Clowns. Three minutes! Line up."

"That's you." Theia gave her a little swat on the behind. "You're on."

Heidi took a deep breath, smoothed her pantaloons, and lifted her chin. "I'm ready."

Theia kissed her goodbye, snuck past the

curtain, and found a place on the steps so she could watch. Minutes passed. The stage stayed bright. Suddenly music surged again through the theater. Mother Ginger clumped across the stage on her stilts, hid a giggle behind her gloved hand and lifted her swaying skirts.

Out cartwheeled five clowns.

Hand. Hand. Foot. Foot.

Each cartwheeling clown landed perfectly.

Heidi tilted her beaming face up toward the lights and began to dance. In her heart, Theia danced alongside her daughter. And perhaps in Heaven, Edna Harkin danced, too, spinning, laughing, landing a cartwheel or two, delighting in the heavenly Father who had brought forth from three generations — daughters, mother, grandmother — His finest legacy of love.

Dear Reader,

How exciting it is to see "The Hair Ribbons" return to print! This novella marks the very beginning of my writing for the Lord. Before this story was ever published, I could feel God working on my heart to make a detour in my career. I felt Him calling me to stop writing romance novels and to start writing stories that helped women understand how greatly the Lord loves them, how worthy they are in His sight, that the Father has a passion and a purpose for everyone. But it seemed as if no Christian publisher wanted my work. My agent and I parted ways.

I hate to tell you about my many months of second-guessing. Am I doing the right thing? Do I really need to move in this direction, or is this a huge mistake? It's as if the Father asked over and over, every time a door slammed in my face, *Do you want to write for Me, Debbi? Do you want to write for Me? Do you REALLY want to write for Me?*

One weekend, while attending a women's retreat with several good friends and fellow writers, everyone talked about their various books and I found myself yearning to produce work that would glorify God. I was so willing! Why wouldn't He use me?

The conference ended on Saturday night, and on Sunday morning a few of us attended Robin Lee Hatcher's church in Boise, Idaho. I'll never forget the moment when Robin turned to me and whispered, "Let's take you to the altar and pray." These dear women, including Karen Bell, then an editor at Multnomah Publishing, gathered around me at the front of this beautiful sanctuary, laid hands on me and prayed for new beginnings in my life. I've never felt so encircled with love and care and certainty. That weekend, at the altar, "The Hair Ribbons" was born.

In the end, Karen Ball was the very editor who bought this first story and gave it an avenue to appear in print. It is based on true happenings here in Jackson Hole. Many of Theia's thoughts and conflicts and hopes came from prayers that we all shared as we prayed for a friend in our Bible study group who was fighting cancer. And the *Nutcracker* scenes come straight from Christmases backstage with my daughter, Avery, red reindeer noses and angel wings and all!

May you be as blessed reading this story as I was by writing it. I wrote "The Hair Ribbons" to help others understand that our victories in life are often made sweeter by the battles God calls us to fight to get to them. May you understand that the Father has a calling and a purpose for your life and that He loves you more than you can ever imagine!

Deborah Bedford

QUESTIONS FOR DISCUSSION

1. How does her mother's experience with breast cancer color Theia's? What made her experience different?

2. How does being a mother influence Theia's approach to her breast cancer? Does she act differently than a woman who didn't have children might? Why or why not?

3. In your childhood what object played the role of the blue hair ribbons? At what point did you set it aside? Why?

4. Theia's doctors talk to her about creating a survival plan. What role should faith play in such a plan? How would you incorporate your faith?

5. Tension pulls Theia's family in different directions. Why does each character rebel/

react in those particular ways? How would you have reacted to a family member's serious illness?

6. What unique support do Theia's daughters provide to her? What is there about the mother-daughter bond that makes their support so invaluable?

■ ■ ■ ■

UNFORGETTABLE
LINDA GOODNIGHT

■ ■ ■ ■

Surely they may forget, yet I will not forget you.
See, I have inscribed you on the palms of my hands.

— *Isaiah* 49:15–16

During the writing of this book, our family suffered the loss of my mother-in-law, Lorene Goodnight. Lorene was more than a mother-in-law. She was the Mom I didn't have. I loved her and she loved me — as mother and daughter. A Christian since the age of twelve (like Frannie), Lorene's steadfast faith and unconditional love taught me a great deal about being a woman of God, lessons I'm still learning. During the last year of her life, this precious saint suffered with a type of dementia. So this book is dedicated to her memory because truly, she may have forgotten many things, but God had not forgotten her. Her name was written in the palms of His hands.

I would also like to acknowledge the many Alzheimer's bloggers, both patients and caregivers, who gave me insight into

your devastating journey. May God be
with you the way He was with Frannie.

CHAPTER ONE

Funny how everything could be normal one minute and utter chaos the next.

For the rest of her life, Carrie Martin would remember that bright Saturday as a perfect spring day in a perfectly happy, settled, safe life.

At ten o'clock in the morning, while on her hands and knees in the front yard transplanting iris bulbs and waiting for her daughter and husband to show up with peat moss from Clifford's Garden Center, Carrie was jolted by the *onk-onk* of a car horn. She didn't need to look up to know who it was, but she did anyway, lifting a dirty gloved hand in greeting as the gold-colored Oldsmobile sailed into the driveway with one final blast of goodwill.

Her mother, the irrepressible Francis Adler — Frannie to her friends — hopped out of the Olds and crossed the grass, her short, green-clad legs pumping with the energy of a woman half her sixty-one years.

Frannie's enormous hat, also green, formed an ever-advancing pool of shade across the sunny lawn. Today was St. Patrick's Day and this was Mother's method of announcing to the world that she was Irish. Even if she hadn't been, she would have worn the hat.

Frannie never did anything halfway.

"Good morning, Mother." Carrie rested back on her heels with a smile.

From behind a pair of mirrored aviator sunglasses, Frannie looked her daughter up and down before extracting a stick-on shamrock from the pocket of her loose cotton jacket — green, of course. "You aren't wearing green."

Well, Mother certainly was.

Frannie slapped the shamrock onto the pocket of Carrie's white camp shirt.

Carrie glanced down. "I am now."

"I saved you from being pinched," her mother said cheerfully. "How do you like my hat?" A pudgy, beringed hand patted the wide brim.

"Very Irish." Like a plump leprechaun. Any minute now Carrie expected her to leap into the air and click her heels. She would do it, too, if the notion struck. As with holidays, Mother never missed an opportunity to have what she termed as fun. Carrie termed it embarrassing.

Take for instance, last year's Gusher Day festivities, their small town's celebration of its oil boom heritage. Mother and her Red Hat Society compatriots, a group of over-fifty ladies with a zest for life, marched in the parade tossing bright red wax lips into the crowd while belting, "Oh What a Beautiful Morning" in a slightly off-key, wobbly-voiced style.

Carrie, watching from the church craft booth, had inwardly cringed at Mother's outrageous display. How could a Christian woman be so . . . boisterous? A better question, perhaps, was how had Francis Adler given birth and parented a daughter who was her total opposite?

Candace Ellis, the pastor's unassuming wife had surprised everyone in the booth by saying, "As soon as I'm old enough, I'm going to join, too. Those ladies have a blast."

Carrie had managed a tight-lipped smile. Not me, she thought. I wouldn't be caught dead prancing in front of everyone in the Red Hat brigade.

She loved her mother, truly, but sometimes she wished her only parent was a little more low-key.

"So, where are you headed this morning,

Mother?" Using the edge of her glove — the only clean spot — to brush hair out of her eyes, Carrie continued to trowel around another overgrown iris. "Or did you come by to help me separate these bulbs?"

"Oh, honey, why don't you let them grow? Your yard would be beautiful filled with all the different-colored irises. Like a rainbow of flowers."

"My yard *is* beautiful," she answered a little stiffly. "Everyone admires the way my flowers border the walkways and line the drive in tidy rows."

She lifted out a tangle of moist, earthy-scented soil and bulbs.

That was the thing about irises. If she wasn't right on them in the spring, rooting them out, they took over. The blessing of course came in giving them away. What she viewed as pests, her friends considered coveted additions to their gardens. Carrie loved her gardens, but she loved them neat and orderly, although she had to admit a certain envy of Mother's carefree attitude about her plants.

She added the uprooted bulbs to the bucket at her knee. Clods of dirt pattered like rain against the thick plastic.

"I think I'll take these over to Sara Perneky." The younger woman had raved about Carrie's garden last spring.

"Wonderful idea." Mother crouched down beside her to peer into the bucket. A fog of Avon cologne mingled with the scent of fresh, fertile earth. "After that nasty divorce, Sara could use a bright spot in her life. Poor girl. Don't let any of these go to waste now. I know half a dozen ladies who would love a start, including me."

"Mother, for goodness' sake. Your garden is overrun now." To Carrie's way of thinking, Mother's garden wasn't a garden. It was a jungle.

"The more the merrier, I always say. Let 'em bloom."

"A perfect nesting place for snakes."

"That could have happened anywhere," Mother said. "Besides, that little critter added a spark to the day. Lots of excitement when a snake comes a-calling."

Dan, Carrie's husband, had been called upon last fall to kill a copperhead found slithering from beneath the jungle of lilac and japonica and honeysuckle vines growing over the concrete top of Mother's cellar. They'd all breathed a sigh of relief afterward when Frannie got out her giant hedge clippers and whacked away the worst of the bushes.

"I wonder where Dan and Lexi are?" Carrie said, shading her eyes to peer down the street. "I thought they'd be back by now."

"Well, fiddle. Lexi's not here?" Frannie adjusted her sunglasses. "I came by to see if she wanted to ride with me to the airport."

Carrie froze. "The airport?"

Riverbend boasted a small airport for private planes. Mostly oilmen flew in and out of there, but occasionally someone gave flying lessons.

"You aren't taking flying lessons, are you?" Frannie had threatened to do just that for years, but money was always an issue. Carrie thanked the good Lord it was. The thought of her mother barnstorming in a single-engine plane gave her hives. She could almost imagine Frannie decked out in Amelia Earhart helmet and goggles taking on a crop dusting job for the express purpose of swooping down to scare her daughter into apoplexy.

Frannie flapped a hand. "Mercy, no. Too expensive."

Fingers gripping the top of the bucket, Carrie didn't realize she was holding her breath until it seeped out in a whistle. "Then whatever for?"

"Skydiving."

Carrie held up a stiff hand, stop sign style.

"You aren't going skydiving, Mother. You aren't."

"Don't get your knickers in a twist, Carrie. The skydiving club is doing a jump today. I'm only going out to watch." A sneaky little grin teased the corners of her vermilion lips. "This time."

Frannie had been threatening to jump out of an airplane as long as Carrie could remember. The idea struck sheer terror in her height-phobic daughter. "Thank the Lord."

Mother checked her watch. "Gotta run. I told Alice I'd stop to pick her up on the way." Alice Sherman was Mother's best friend.

"Are you coming by later?"

"Probably not, honey. I have bowling tonight."

Carrie lifted an eyebrow. "With Ken?"

She liked teasing her mother about the rugged farmer. The pair had been friends long before Ken's wife died, but now Carrie suspected a romance. Except for the fact that Ken had taught Frannie to drive a tractor and ride a horse, both a little silly for someone of her age, Carrie was glad. Mother had been alone for most of her life.

Fran flapped a hand and laughed, her cheeks shining pink as she headed toward the gold Olds, or as Lexi called it, The Tanker. "Tell Lexi she missed out."

"Are you still coming for dinner tomorrow after church?"

Her mother stopped, turned and whipped off her aviator sunglasses. "I'd forgotten all about it."

Carrie squelched a twinge of irritation that she was low man on Mother's totem pole. "Are you coming? I'm baking a red velvet cake."

"Wouldn't miss it, then." She shoved the sunglasses back in place. "And honey, why don't you take those extra bulbs over to Sara Perneky? She could use some good cheer."

Before Carrie could remind her mother that they'd already discussed doing exactly that, Frannie had slammed the car door and cranked the engine.

As the Olds roared away, Mother gave two final blasts of the horn.

Carrie waved, shaking her head. Mother was . . . well, Mother.

By the time Dan and Lexi returned with the peat moss along with a bag of burgers from Whopper World and a few other items Carrie didn't remember needing, Carrie had gone inside for a break.

"Saw your mom at Wal-Mart." Dan bent to kiss her cheek.

"That's funny. Mother stopped by more than an hour ago and didn't say a word about seeing you." Carrie dipped to the side so as not to streak Dan's green Henley with dirt and shoved her hands under the kitchen faucets. Her back ached a little from muscles atrophied by winter. "She wanted Lexi to go with her."

"Where?" Lexi asked, though she continued rummaging through a Wal-Mart bag.

"The airport to watch skydiving." Carrie rinsed her hands and reached toward the paper towel holder. "I didn't know you were going to Wal-Mart."

No wonder they'd been gone so long.

"Lexi needed some new earrings."

"Oh right. Like my mother needs another hat."

"I didn't have any blue ones." Lexi tilted her head to display a series of neon-colored hoops dangling below two gleaming studs. "Do you like them, Mom?"

They were hideous. Three holes in one ear. Good grief. "Great for spring."

"You hate them."

Carrie patted her daughter's silky brown hair. At fifteen and all legs, Lexi was growing into a beauty with tastes of her own.

She was a great kid. The only kid. Though Carrie and Dan had prayed for more, these prayers had gone unanswered. "If you like them, that's all that matters."

"I told Dad you'd say that." Her daughter didn't seem the least offended. Their tastes had never run along the same lines and lately the gulf had widened. Where Carrie preferred subtle and classic, Lexi gravitated toward bold colors and the hottest trends.

"Come on." Lexi settled at the bar. "Let's eat. I'm starving."

Dan pulled a face. "This is after two doughnuts."

Even with starbursts bracketing his eyes from years of working out in the sun, Dan Martin was a handsome man, fit and trim with hair as dark as ever. His worst flaw was that he didn't attend church and in a small town like Riverbend, church membership was socially important. Though Dan claimed to be a believer, he also claimed to spend more time with God in the great outdoors than most people did in church. Carrie wasn't much on the long-winded preaching, but she'd made plenty of friends and hopefully some brownie points with God by working in the nursery every single service for the past ten years.

"You stopped at the bakery, too?" Paper

rustled as she took a fragrant burger from a sack and straddled a bar stool. "I'm starting to feel left out."

Dan shot her a wink. "Brought you a surprise."

Dan's bakery surprise was always the same. "If it's a chocolate éclair, you'll be forgiven, although I may change my mind when I go shopping for an Easter dress."

"You look good to me."

Mouth full of burger and heart full of pleasure, Carrie was laughing with her lips closed when the telephone rang. Lexi exploded off the bar. "I got it."

In seconds she was back, holding the cordless receiver toward her mother. "For you."

At Carrie's questioning look, she shrugged and mouthed, "I don't know," then poked another ketchup-laden French fry into her mouth.

Carrie quickly swallowed and put her sandwich down. "Hello?"

"Mrs. Martin?"

"Yes, who's this?"

"Officer Shane Wallace with the Riverbend police department."

Carrie's nerves tensed. The bar's granite felt cold against her elbow. "Hello, Shane. Is something wrong?"

Shane's family attended her church. One

of the perks of small town living was being acquainted with at least one person in every sector of business and government.

"Yes, ma'am, I'm afraid there is. I'm here with Mrs. Adler, your mother. I thought I should call you first."

Carrie blinked. First? Before what?

Her hand tightened on the receiver. She looked at Dan, who had lowered his hamburger and now watched her with curiosity.

"Has she had an accident?"

"No, ma'am." My, he was formal today. "At least, none that we can ascertain. You see, I found her sitting in her car on the shoulder of Highway 56. When I stopped to assist she didn't recognize me."

"Oh, well, that's understandable. You look so grown-up in your uniform."

"You don't understand. Mrs. Adler seems confused. She didn't know where she was, how she got here or where she was going."

Carrie brushed a stray hair out of her eyes. Her shoulders relaxed the tiniest bit. "Are you sure Mother isn't teasing you, Shane? You know how she loves to joke around."

"I don't think so, Mrs. Martin. Your mom seems pretty scared."

Mother? Scared? Impossible. Mother was fearless. Nothing scared her. She'd raised two children single-handedly on a pauper's wages. Two years ago she'd trekked the jungles of Honduras to take supplies and Bibles to a group of native churches. Mother had never expressed fear about anything. Ever.

"But she was here only a while ago and everything was fine. I just don't understand . . ."

"Mrs. Martin," the young officer's voice intruded, this time with a respectful firmness. "I really think you should come."

"Oh." Suddenly, the call was too real. Something *was* wrong. "Okay. Yes. Of course I will. Tell me what to do."

Carrie took note of Shane's instructions and then replaced the receiver. She felt numb. Not scared. Numb.

"Carrie?" Dan had appeared from somewhere to touch her arm. "Who was that, honey? You're as pale as paper."

"We have to go. Let me get my purse. Something's happened to Mother." Her fingers clawed into Dan's forearm. "Oh, Dan, I'm afraid Mother's had a stroke."

CHAPTER TWO

"It's probably one of those mini strokes," Carrie said for the tenth time. She sat in the waiting room outside the Emergency Room, shivering from nerves and the overhead air-conditioning vent. Her fingers twisted the handle of her purse into a knot. "I've heard of those. A person has a tiny lapse in memory. It's not all that uncommon or even serious. Mother will be fine. I'm sure."

Dan, his wide shoulders uncomfortably crammed onto a too-small swoop of green plastic the hospital considered seating, patted her knee. From the time they'd arrived, she'd prattled on like a magpie. He was probably sick of listening, but she couldn't help it. Nothing could be wrong with Mother. She was invincible.

Carrie pulled air into her lungs, the clean, antiseptic smell reassuring in some bizarre way. Cleanliness was next to godliness. If she was clean, she was godly and nothing bad could happen.

Tempted to laugh aloud at the race of silly thoughts, Carrie wondered if she was getting hysterical. Heaven forbid.

"The doctor will write her one of those new prescriptions for cholesterol or blood thinners or whatever they are," she went on, unable to stop the flow of words. "You see them advertised on TV all the time. A prescription and she'll be fine."

"We don't even know if it is a stroke yet, Carrie." Dan reminded her, his tone gentle. Maybe too gentle. It made her even more nervous. Her throat went as dry as a saltine.

"Of course it's a stroke. What else could cause her to forget where she was?"

Shane, the police officer who'd called, had stayed around only long enough to be respectful and then he'd left. Business at the small town E.R. was surprisingly fast paced. Carrie couldn't remember the last time she'd been here. Maybe when Lexi wrecked her bike and needed stitches, but that had been five years ago.

Times changed.

The thought frightened her. If times changed, people changed. They got sick. They died. She closed her eyes momentarily against the inevitable decline of human be-

193

ings. Morbid thoughts. An overreaction, surely, to being in an emergency room. She hated hospitals.

Two nurses swished by in a rush, stethoscopes swaying. Croc shoes instead of white orthopedics squished softly on white tile that had been polished to a mirror finish. The intercom beeped for some doctor she'd never heard of. When had Riverbend grown large enough for strange doctors?

She angled toward her husband, deeply relieved that he'd come with her. "Do you think we should call Lexi?"

Dan swiveled his head in her direction, his eyes as calm and gray-blue as Lake Placid. "And tell her what?"

That was Dan. Solid. Quiet. Irritatingly calm. He hadn't even gotten excited the day a tornado ripped the roof off their storage building.

"I don't know. She must be worried."

Though fifteen and well able to remain home alone, as the only grandchild living in the same state, Lexi was very close to her beloved "Grannie Frannie" and would be waiting by the telephone.

Without further comment, Dan took their shared cell phone from her purse and punched in numbers. They'd never seen any reason to own two. It seemed extravagant, as did the notion of using a cell phone to take camera photos or for text messaging. She'd learned from Frannie the importance of frugality, though as a teenager she had been humiliated by their tiny family's poverty.

The three of them, including her younger brother, Robby, had struggled by on the minimum wages paid to a widow without a high school diploma. A few times, when things had gotten particularly difficult, Carrie suspected Mother had taken public assistance in order to provide for them, though she'd never admitted as much to her children. Carrie was humiliated just thinking about it, and had vowed never to let that happen to her.

The tightness in Carrie's chest increased. Mother's life had not been easy.

Dear God, let her be all right. Like all her thoughts today, the prayer was half-baked. If you'll let her be all right, I promise to work harder at getting Dan into church. I promise —

An exam door opened. "Mr. and Mrs. Martin?" A smiling nurse looked in their direction and motioned them inside. "You can come in now. The doctor will be with you as soon as he can."

Dan poked one thick finger at the phone,

discontinuing the call to Lexi. "I'll call her after we see Fran."

Clutching her purse against her waist, Carrie jerked upright. With dismay, she realized she still wore the white camp blouse, complete with peeling shamrock and smudges of dirt. The knees of her old cotton gardening slacks were grass stained. Fervently, she hoped no one from work or church saw her here.

Dan touched her elbow. "Carrie?"

She nodded, swallowing. "She must be fine. The nurse is smiling."

With Dan at her side, she rushed into the exam room. Frannie sat on the side of a paper-covered table humming, high-heeled feet swinging as if she had not a care in the world.

Carrie stopped short. "Mother, are you all right? What in the world happened? You scared us half to death. Shane said you were confused, didn't know where you were or how you got there."

Her mother stopped humming. Head tilted to one side, a tiny frown puckered between well-penciled eyebrows, she asked, "Shane? Was that who that was? Shane Wallace? I thought he looked familiar but I couldn't place him. Such a nice young man."

"You've known Shane since he was born, Mother."

"Hand me my hat. I feel naked." Frannie's green, broad-brimmed hat occupied the only chair in the room. Carrie took up the monstrosity and handed it over. "I had a senior moment, that's all. I'm fine and dandy now." She perched the wide felt atop her fluffed hair and gave it a pat for emphasis. "Let's go home."

"Not until we talk to the doctor."

"I talked to him. No need for you to bother." Frannie hopped down from the table and glanced at her watch. "Fiddle. I've missed the skydiving. Alice will be disappointed. She's sweet on Rick Chambers, you know, and he looks really cute in his jumpsuit." She pumped her eyebrows up and down.

"Mother, for goodness' sake. Something happened to you today and we are not going to sweep it under the rug." But as she spoke, her anxiety eased toward relief. Maybe nothing had happened. Maybe the episode really was just a senior moment. Sometimes she jumped to conclusions. She had a tendency to expect the worst because she'd learned the hard way that life usually handed out lemons and no one she knew had a lemonade stand. "Tell me what the doctor said?"

"He said I'm a hoot and he liked my hat. I gave him a shamrock. All that white-coat business hurt my eyes."

"Mother! I am not leaving here until I talk to him." Carrie spun toward the door, willing and able to block the entrance if her mother tried to leave before that doctor arrived. "Where is he anyway?"

"Carrie." Dan's voice held a note of warning. He was always like that, reminding his impatient wife to wait and see. Sometimes, like today, his accepting attitude was downright annoying.

A rebuke boiled up on her tongue but died away when the physician, looking young enough to be in high school, sailed into the room. In a crisp white lab coat and a blue tie, he carried a large brown envelope tucked beneath one arm. Frannie's shamrock was squarely in place over his heart.

"Where's Dr. Morrison?" Carrie asked, caught off guard and not at all comfortable with a green-behind-the-ears college boy. Dr. Morrison had cared for her family for fifteen years. He knew Frannie and all her idiosyncrasies. He would know if something was seriously wrong.

"Taking some time off. I'm Dr. Wilson." He extended his hand, first to her and then to Dan. "And yes, I graduated from medical school. I'm not as young as I look."

Mollified but a bit embarrassed, Carrie nodded stiffly.

"What's wrong with my mother? Did she have a stroke?" Her stomach rumbled in memory of the half-eaten hamburger. Carrie pressed a hand to her midsection.

Dr. Wilson hitched the leg of his expertly creased slacks and perched on the edge of the gurney. The doctor gazed at Frannie standing next to him like a chubby green bird about to take flight. She winked at him. He smiled and turned his attention to Carrie. "I've already discussed my concerns with Ms. Adler —"

"Mother, why didn't you just tell us?"

"Tell you what, honey?"

With a heavy, exasperated sigh to let Fran know she was annoyed, Carrie looked to the doctor for clarity. "What is it, Doctor?"

"I want to run some further tests and consult with a neurologist."

Prickles rose on the back of Carrie's neck. "A neurologist? For what?"

Frannie answered for him. "Alzheimer's, honey. The doctor thinks I'm losing my mind."

Three weeks and many clinic visits later

Fran sat across the desk from a neurologist who looked as if he'd flavored his coffee with pickle juice.

Carrie sat next to her, face stony and pale as the doctor confirmed the diagnosis. She'd known he would. That's why she hadn't wanted Carrie to come, but here she was, shaking like a leaf and looking the way she had when she was ten and ate too many green blackberries. Sick and hollow-eyed.

Fran understood the feeling. She was feeling a little sick herself. Jittery, too. No one wanted to be told that she would eventually disappear into a fog and break her family's hearts.

"Isn't there a medicine for it?" Carrie's fingers trembled as she pushed her hair behind one ear.

Of all the things Fran had dreaded about today, this was the worst, to know her family would suffer because of her, and there was so little she could do about it.

Dr. Pickle Juice made a few more comments, then excused himself and left. A nurse came in, smiling more than the doctor, and handed them both a card about the Alzheimer's Association. Frannie gave her a Jesus Loves You smiley sticker, and slid the card into her I Love NY purse. She'd never been to New York, but she'd always wanted to go. Maybe she would do that now. Someday was no longer an option.

"I don't know what to do," Carrie said when they were alone.

Fran placed a hand on her daughter's arm. "We do what we've always done. We put it in the Lord's hands and trust Him."

The look Carrie gave her said she didn't buy that answer in the least.

The ugly diagnosis haunted Carrie day and night. She could think of little else. Mother's casual attitude didn't help, either. Carrie wondered if denial, nonchalance and a foolish determination to put a happy face on a devastating diagnosis were symptoms of the disease. An hour after they'd arrived home from the clinic Mother changed into a rhinestone cowboy hat and red boots and went to her weekly guitar lesson. How foolish was that?

Robby, Carrie's brother, was no help. Though concerned, he lived in Michigan and couldn't grasp the seriousness of the situation. He'd said Mom sounded fine to him when they'd spoken on the phone. She knew how he felt. Denial was easier than reality.

"Until now, I never even realized anything was wrong," Carrie told Dan one night as they sat on the patio staring up at an April moon. The evening air was chilly so they huddled under a fleece throw. Instead of the usual romantic snuggle, the air hung heavy with Carrie's worry. "She's always been outrageous and silly. Who would notice if she forgot an appointment or repeated herself? I forgot to call the insurance company about that wind damage to the roof and there's nothing wrong with me."

She said the last as if it worried her, because it did.

"Everyone forgets things," Dan agreed, his thick, calloused fingertips making lazy circles on her shoulder.

"The neurologist says she may not get bad for a long time. No one can really predict. In fact, he can't even be one hundred percent sure she has Alzheimer's disease. Mother keeps saying she's fine, that she and God will beat this thing."

"Your mom is a strong woman."

Carrie made a little noise in the back of her throat. "You can say that again. No one ties down the irrepressible Frannie."

No *person* could, but this ugly disease with a German name eventually would. Bile rose in the back of Carrie's throat, as bitter as the feeling in her soul.

"I don't understand God," she muttered,

gazing up at the marbled-cheese moon. She had grown up without a father, and now she was going to lose her mother in the most heinous manner. Where was God in any of that? "Old lady Smith across the street is a mean, bitter old hag who never contributes to anything and wouldn't call 9-1-1 if you died in her living room. But she's still sharp as a tack and making everyone miserable while a vibrant, giving woman like Mother is struck down in her prime. If there was any justice, Ms. Smith would get Alzheimer's. Not Mother."

Dan squeezed the side of her neck but said nothing. That was Dan. Sometimes she longed for him to hash things out with her, to argue or debate or just talk something into the ground, but he never did. No matter how big the problem, Dan kept his thoughts to himself. It was a wonder the man didn't explode. She would have.

Especially now when she was angry and confused and depressed.

Mother's life had never been easy. Only in the last few years had everything settled into a pleasant rhythm. Mother loved her job as church secretary. Her house, though only a small frame structure with two bedrooms, was paid for and she'd been saving money for another missions adventure, as she called them. This time to help with a Bible camp for orphans.

Yes, after all Mother had done for the Lord, Alzheimer's disease was a lousy method of repayment.

CHAPTER THREE

Ken Markovich's farm smelled like fresh-mowed grass with just the hint of the red, muddy river which gave Riverbend its name. Bottomland, people around here called the area. Rich, fertile farmland that would grow about anything. Fran loved coming out here where the birds pecked at plowed ground, and it wasn't unusual to see a red fox chasing mice across the fields. Once she'd lain on her belly in the grass and watched a mama coyote teach her young to catch grasshoppers. It was the cutest thing.

"You're quiet today." Ken walked beside her toward the horse corral. He didn't have a lot of animals, but he loved buckskin horses and kept several to ride for enjoyment and in parades. He looked so handsome decked out in cowboy hat and chaps riding astride a big, muscled gelding. "Anything wrong?"

The feeling of dread that had hovered over her all day settled low in her belly.

"I've been praying about something." As hard as this was, she had to tell him. He deserved to know. She'd barely slept last night, praying and thinking and trying to decide the best way to break the news.

"Need any help?" The question was one of the many things she loved about Ken. They shared a common dependence on the Lord. For both of them, God was a friend as well as their Lord and Savior. Talking to Him was as natural as breathing.

"I need to tell you something. Something important."

She followed him through the gate, thinking what a good man he was. He wasn't hard to look at, either. His hair had gone white a long time ago along with his mustache, but his eyebrows and lashes were a gorgeous contrast in black.

"I'm listening."

A mare plodded forward to greet them. Ken crooked an arm over her back and leaned on the shiny coat. Frannie rubbed the soft muzzle, felt the moist breath from the mare's velvety nostrils against her skin.

Every sensation seemed more precious now that she knew she'd someday forget the simple pleasures.

"I've been seeing a doctor."

Ken straightened, his arm dropping to his side. She could see the wheels turning, could almost smell his anxiety. "Is it —"

She shook her head. "Not cancer."

A visible quiver of relief ran through him. "Thank the Lord Jesus."

"Yes. I'm grateful for that, too, but the news is not very good." She swallowed, nervous again, her stomach pitching like sea waves. She'd meant to say something funny and make him laugh first, but nothing came to mind. "Remember those times I've had difficulty talking? And that night at clogging when I got upset because I'd lost my purse but it was right where I'd left it?"

"I remember." His curious concern was edged with wariness. "What's going on, Fran?"

"I have early-onset Alzheimer's, the forgetting disease."

Shock registered on his face. Shock and fear.

A tractor rumbled and rattled in a distant field, stirring up a cloud of dust. A horsefly buzzed the mare. She stomped her foot and the fly buzzed off. Frannie wanted to do the same. Stomp her foot and shoo away the truth.

"Is there anything I can do?"

"Not a thing except be my friend." She'd settle for friendship now, though they'd been more for a long time.

Ken nodded, looking as if the mare had kicked him in the gut. She knew the feeling.

"Get that sad look off your face, Ken Markovich." She swatted his arm, playfully, and forced cheer into her words. "I've always been a little crazy, so what's the big deal, right?"

He managed a sickly smile. "Right."

A pulse quivered in her throat, making her breathless. He was upset, as she'd known he would be, but she also felt him pulling back, retreating from her, as though she'd announced a case of leprosy. The notion ached inside her.

She straightened her hat, a wide-brimmed bonnet in turquoise with peacock feathers arching from the back. "I'll need your prayers, you know."

"Sure, sure. You got 'em." He shifted uncomfortably. "This is a hard thing, Frannie. I'm sorry. You're too good for this." He shook his head. "I don't know what to do. I don't even know what to say."

Nor did she.

The two of them had never been at a loss for words, but now they stood with the painful news throbbing between, both lost in thought, and neither able to say what the other needed to hear. She wasn't sure what she'd expected from Ken, but she had no words of reassurance and neither did he.

Frannie waved away an imaginary gnat, sick at heart. Sick in mind. "Well, I guess I should go. Lexi has a ball game tonight."

Ken scratched at his mustache. "Can't miss that."

"You coming?"

"This time of year is really busy, the hay and all." His eyes slid away from hers. "You know how it is."

A beat passed while Fran studied his beloved burnished face. He was afraid. So was she. Maybe he just needed time to think, to process the news.

Lord, losing my mind is hard. Don't let me lose my friends, too.

"Yes," she said finally. "I know how it is."

Heart heavy, Fran walked away.

Hands deep in suds, squeezing Woolite in and out of her favorite sweaters, Carrie heard a car pull up. Wednesday was her day off from the library, and she'd determined to get all her winter things cleaned and organized into clear storage boxes today. Using her shoulder to scratch the inevitable nose itch, she stuck her head between the snow-white Cape Cod swags.

Frannie popped out of The Tanker and slammed the door, the metallic echo coming right through the walls. Dressed in snug blue capris that turned her hips to anvils and a bluer baseball cap, her short legs pumped across Dan's manicured lawn like squatty pistons.

As happened every time she saw her mother since that awful day at the neurologist's office, Carrie's stomach nose-dived. The more she tried not to consider what was to come, the worse her imaginings.

Mother tried to put on a happy face and pretend all was well, an obvious act that angered Carrie. Not that she was angry with her mother, but she was most definitely angry.

She squinted into the sunlight. What was Mother carrying? Papers?

The question was answered before she could rinse her hands and reach for a paper towel. Frannie breezed in and slapped a thick stack of eight and a half-by-fourteen documents onto the granite bar. Legal documents.

"All done," she announced, jaw unusually set in a face normally as mobile as a child's.

Carrie crossed the kitchen and rounded the bar to peer over her mother's shoulder.

"What is all this?"

"My house is officially in order," she said, as matter-of-fact as if announcing she'd bought a bunch of broccoli for dinner. "Power of attorney goes to you, of course. Robby lives too far away. Everything is done so you won't have to make the decisions — right down to my funeral. I want a trumpet to play 'When the Saints Go Marching In,' lots of laughs and hallelujahs, a real joy-of-the-Lord send-off. None of that whining, snot-slinging business."

"Mother, what are you talking about?" She would love to have blamed the onset of dementia for her mother's chatter, but Fran Adler had been this way as long as Carrie could remember.

"While I still have my senses about me, I want to make the decisions. So I did. The papers are here. Put them up somewhere until you need them. You'll know when. The copies are in my safe-deposit box, which is now in your name as well as mine, along with my house, car, and the little dab of money stuck away in savings."

"Oh." The cold chill of reality seeped deep into Carrie's bones as she flipped through the stack of papers. Mother had left no stone unturned, including a do-not-resuscitate order. Carrie jerked her hand away from that one. "You didn't need to do this yet, Mother. For goodness' sake! You're still in command of your faculties."

"For the most part, yes, but I'm slipping."

"You are not. Stop talking about it." Carrie whirled away from the bar and started opening and shutting cabinet doors with more force than necessary. Throat tight and thick, she fought down the fury that hovered on the edge of her emotions all the time lately. This whole Alzheimer's thing was wrong. Unfair.

Life stunk. No matter how hard a person worked and tried, there was always something lurking around the corner to knock the wind out of you.

Reaching inside a cabinet, she yanked at a Tupperware bowl. A flood of plastic lids tumbled out, splatting all over the floor and counter and even into the sink where one floated atop her pink silk twin set.

"Carrie Ann, listen to me, honey." Mother's voice came from behind. "Quit flitting around the kitchen like a housefly afraid of getting swatted. I'm trying to be sensible while I can. Neither of us can escape the truth."

Carrie gripped the countertop with both hands and stared at the diamond pattern of the tiled backsplash. The grout needed cleaning. She bent to the cabinet below and reached for the Tilex. "We don't have to talk about it all the time."

Mother's hands, strong from a lifetime of busyness, gripped her shoulders and forced her up. "Your grout is fine, Carrie Ann, as spotless as everything in your life except me. And Tilex will not fix what's happening in my brain. Sit down. Every time I try to bring up the subject, you start cleaning something. Today we're talking. No cleaning. Do you have any Mountain Dew?"

"No." Carrie slumped into one of the Queen Anne side chairs.

"No Mountain Dew?" Mother huffed as if insulted. "Iced tea then."

She retrieved the filled pitcher Carrie kept available in case of company, poured two glasses, plunked them down and then sat, too.

"I've known something was wrong for a long time," Mother said without preamble. "Now the problem has a name. We can plan for it and deal with it."

Carrie stared into the amber-colored tea and absently slid a finger and thumb up and down the damp glass. She didn't want to hear this, but she was too old to run away and hide in the back of the closet to avoid facing unpleasantness. Hiding hadn't worked for her at ten, and it wouldn't work at forty-two.

"You never said a word."

"What could I say? I hoped I was experiencing normal forgetfulness. Where were my keys, my reading glasses, that kind of thing. Then I started getting confused at work, mixing up files and phone numbers. One day I was talking on the telephone and got so confused, I hung up. I knew what I wanted to say but the words wouldn't come out right."

"I didn't know," Carrie said past the ache in her throat. Her mother had been in trouble and she hadn't even noticed. "I thought you were being your usual goofy yourself."

Frannie's eyes widened in mirth. "It helps being crazy in advance."

"Don't, Mother. Please don't."

Fannie patted the back of her hand. "Okay, if it makes you feel better. Laughter's good medicine, though. That's Bible. Wise old King Solomon himself said that. Anyway, back to this forgetting thing. I thought I was overdoing, tired, whatever, so I tried getting more sleep, taking vitamins. I even started taking cod-liver oil because it's supposed to be brain food. Can you imagine?"

Carrie squinched her eyes and shuddered. "Yuck."

"Yuck is right, and the nasty stuff didn't do anything but make the cat want to lick my face." Frannie grinned, but the emotion didn't reach her eyes. Her lipstick had faded with the day, leaving the rim of red liner.

Carrie had a horrible thought that her mother would be like this. All the color and vibrance fading away with only the outer shadow left behind.

She took a sip of the cold drink in an effort to wash down the dark taste of sorrow. Mother may be putting on a happy face but Carrie couldn't.

The ice maker rumbled and the clock on the stove ticked once. Her mother took a deep breath, held it, held it, held it and then slowly exhaled.

"I was in the hardware store yesterday and not only forgot why I was there but what kind of store it was. I kept looking around at tools and light fixtures and wondering if someone was having a garage sale." She made a self-deprecating sound through her nose. "Isn't that silly? It's like this cloud comes over my brain, then after a while moves on, letting the sun back in. It's the weirdest feeling." Her voice dwindled to a stop like a car slowly running out of gas.

"Oh, Mother." Carrie leaned her forehead onto the heel of her hand. *Why God? Why are You doing this?*

Frannie sipped at her tea and grimaced. "Unsweetened. You should have warned me." She plunked the glass down and swiped at the condensation ring on the table. "You know what I discovered in my cupboards last night?"

Carrie shook her head. "I'm not sure I want to know."

"Twenty-two cans of chicken noodle soup." Frannie slapped her thigh and cackled. "What do you think? Maybe I was expecting a flu epidemic?"

How could Mother laugh when Carrie wanted to run screaming from the kitchen. "How did that happen?"

"I don't know. Well, I do, actually. When I would go shopping, I'd wonder if I was out of soup, but I wasn't sure so I bought more. Guess what else I stocked up on?"

"Do I dare ask?"

"Eight bottles of ketchup, nine giant jars of dill pickles and — get this — sixteen cans of creamed corn."

"You don't even like creamed corn."

"No, but Lexi does. That child can eat creamed corn like most kids eat peanut butter and jelly. I guess I didn't want to disap-

216

point her by running out."

"Oh, Mother," Carrie said again, voice as heavy as her heart.

"I know, honey," Frannie said, patting her shoulder. "At least I know today. I may forget in ten minutes but I know right now. Someday I'll be able to hide my own Easter eggs."

"Stop it! Stop joking about this. There is nothing funny about Alzheimer's disease."

Expression mild, Frannie answered, "No, there isn't, but this is my new reality. I can face it with a smile or a frown, but I have to face it. The Lord has always taken care of us, Carrie. We have to trust that He's in this, too."

Yeah, well, if He was in this thing, Carrie would like to know where. How could Mother go on blithely trusting a God who was letting her down in the worst possible way? If He cared at all, He could stop this awful thing from happening to a woman who had served Him all the days of her life. *If* He cared.

Carrie shoved away from the table and stalked to the kitchen sink to yank the drain plug.

Frannie followed her, heeled slides tip-tapping on the tile. "I told Dr. Morrison to put me on the list for trials and drugs tests and anything experimental."

"Oh, like that's going to cheer me up."

Swishing the pink sweaters up and down while running a blast of cold rinse water, Carrie had a vision of her mother with probes and electrodes poking from her head like Frankenstein. Knowing Frannie, she'd probably wear the conglomeration like a hat and march down the street in the Independence Day Parade.

"If I have to have this silly forgetting disease, I want somebody to get some good out of it. If not me, someone else. God can take this bad thing and bring something good from it the way He always does. Besides, I like the idea of being a pioneer," she said, cheerfully. "Just think, Carrie, if they could find a cure through me. Wouldn't that be magnificent?"

Magnificent would be if Mother didn't have this disease in the first place.

"Would you hand me that towel over there?" And stop talking about this. "I want to get these sweaters laid out to dry before Lexi comes home from school."

The front door banged opened. "Mom!"

"Too late." Frannie smiled, handing over the thick, terry towel. "Our girl is home." Cupping her hands around her mouth like parentheses, she called, "In here, rosebud."

Dropping books and a one-strap backpack as she came, Lexi rounded the bar. "Hi, Grannie Frannie."

Frannie produced a cheek for smooching, and Carrie did the same. Lexi looped her arms around Carrie's shoulders for a hug, her slim-as-a-rail body pressed into her mother's back. She smelled of Sea Island Cotton by Bath & Body Works along with freshly applied strawberry lip gloss and that special scent found only in public schools. Her sleek brown hair, lightened like a halo around her angelic face, brushed softly against Carrie's cheek.

For the first time all afternoon, Carrie's mood lifted. Dear Lord, she loved this child. While other mothers bemoaned their teenagers, Carrie felt almost smug about her close-to-perfect daughter. She was good at mothering, a fact that still caused a yearning for the children she'd never had.

"Do you have softball practice today?" Frannie asked.

Lexi smooched Carrie's cheek again and straightened. "Yes. Want to take me out for pizza first?"

Mother's baseball cap bobbed. "Sounds like fun."

Carrie tensed. Given this afternoon's talk, the idea of her mother venturing off with her only child was not welcome. Yes, they'd run around together for years like two best friends, but things were different now.

Lexi opened the fridge, took out a carrot and crunched. "Is it okay if we pick up Courtney?"

"You bet. Tell her to bring that bong-bong CD."

Carrie turned from the sink, hands dripping. "Bong-bong?"

Lexi's shoulders hunched into giggle. "That's what Grannie Frannie calls hip-hop."

"Ah."

"Go change clothes and get your gear." Mother's hands made a shooing motion. "I'm raring to go."

"You're the best granny ever." After a final, quick hug, Lexi started out of the kitchen, half-eaten carrot in hand. "Wait'll you see my new batting gloves, Grannie Frannie. They're so cool. Hot pink and purple. Courtney has the same ones."

Carrie waited until Lexi was out of hearing range. "I'm not sure this is such a good idea."

Mother, still smiling in Lexi's direction, slowly turned to face Carrie. "Why not?"

Carrie clutched the wet towel in her hands like a life preserver. "Did the doctor say you could continue to drive?"

"Of course. He said I'd know when to stop."

That wasn't too reassuring. "What if you have another lapse?"

Mother's smile dwindled away. "Carrie, I've driven all over the county since the diagnosis. No problems at all. Besides, Lexi will be with me."

That's what worried her. She bit her bottom lip in an effort to keep her mouth shut.

But Mother knew her too well. "I'd never do anything to endanger our girl."

"Not intentionally."

"All right, I hear that tone of voice. You don't want her to ride with me, do you?"

Feeling small, Carrie nodded. "I'm sorry, Mother. I'd rather she didn't."

She should have expected the hurt on her mother's face, but the look of betrayal hit her hard.

Frannie's mouth sagged, then tightened with decision. "I'll go talk to her."

As she watched her mother leave the kitchen with less than the usual zip in her step, Carrie felt like the worst daughter on earth. But what else could she do? She had to protect her only child.

Chapter Four

"Lord, I'm worried about Carrie."

Fran knelt beside her bed. Her tomcat, Tux, lay curled on the pillow above her head, listening with sleepy-eyed disinterest. She'd been here more than usual lately and God always met her, His sweet spirit pouring strength and love into her often frightened being.

For the last thirty minutes, she'd prayed for Ken. He hadn't called, hadn't come by. So she prayed not to be hurt or angry, prayed for understanding. Understanding had finally come when the Lord brought to mind Emily Markovich and her ravaging cancer. For three years Ken had helplessly watched disease eat away at his wife. No man deserved to go through that twice. Though sad to lose his love and friendship, Fran accepted that he simply could not face such an uncertain future.

Now she'd turned her thoughts to her

family, particularly Carrie.

"She's having such a hard time with this little problem of mine. Lord, my fondest wish has always been to see her full of Your joy and living in Your extravagant love and grace. But she's unhappy, angry even, and I fear she's angry with You. Forgive her, Jesus, and help her. Somehow I've failed her. Failed to be the example I should have been. Failed to show her that Your grace is everywhere if she'll only look. Forgive me, Lord Jesus, forgive me, and teach me how to help her before it's too late, before my mind is gone and I'm no good to anyone."

Tears clogged the back of her throat. She refused to cry for herself, but the thought of her child, struggling and hurting, broke her in half.

"This latest thing is going to upset her even more, Father. I'm okay with it. Really, I am. Your grace is sufficient. But You know Carrie. She'll have a fit. And I don't know how to break the news."

Careful not to dislodge the child on her lap, Carrie closed the book she was reading and turned the cover so the half circle of pre-schoolers sitting around her on the red-and-blue alphabet rug could see the art. "And that, children, is the story of *Red Fish, Blue*

Fish by Dr. Seuss. Wasn't that fun?"

"Weed it again," came one small voice.

Carrie smiled down into a pair of big brown eyes. "Our time is up for today. Perhaps your mother will check it out for you to take home. And you can ask her to bring you back for story time on Saturday morning. Okay?"

The child's head bobbed up and down. Then he popped up from the rug and made a beeline for an approaching woman Carrie knew to be his mother.

She enjoyed working at the library, loved the order and the quiet and the smell of books. But most of all, she loved reading to the little ones.

The toddler on her lap popped a wet thumb out of his mouth and grinned at her. Her heart turned over. What she wouldn't have given to have borne more children. Since adolescence, she'd dreamed of at least three, maybe four, two boys and two girls. When they'd married, Dan had wanted a large family, too, and as the years slid by, Carrie's feeling of failure had grown because she'd never been able to give him one. A rugged, outdoorsman like Dan naturally wanted a son, though being Dan he'd never complained after her failing became obvious. Though they'd prayed and prayed for more children after Lexi, none ever came.

So now, to satisfy her nurturer's heart, Carrie grew flowers, loved her only child, kept the church nursery and read to other people's children twice a week.

"Miss Carrie." A towheaded blonde in a dinosaur T-shirt tugged on her sleeve. "I got a new kitty."

"You did?" Carrie shifted the child in her arms, but didn't put him down. Having a little one snuggled warm and trusting against her felt good and filled a need she couldn't voice. "Why, Jamie, that's wonderful. What's her name?"

"She's a boy," Jamie said with four-year-old wisdom. "Her name is Killer 'cause Daddy said she better kill mice or she's a dead duck." He squinted at her mouth. "Have you gots any gum?"

Carrie laughed and patted the boy's bony shoulder. "Sorry, Jamie. No gum allowed in the library. Remember?"

The children began to move away, some to the large, spongy blocks, some to the thick board books, and others to rejoin their waiting mothers. Reluctantly, Carrie relinquished the toddler to a young brunette who looked barely old enough to drive.

"He's precious." Carrie smoothed a hand over the child's soft brown hair.

"Thanks." The mother, large with yet another baby, took the toddler's hand and smiled in return. Carrie refused to acknowledge the pinch of envy. She was forty-two, for goodness' sake. Far past the age to wish for babies.

Carrie waited until all the children had been reunited with their parents and then rose from the stuffed reading chair and began reshelving books.

As she bent for a copy of *Goodnight Moon*, a woman she knew from church approached.

"I've been waiting to ask you, Carrie. How's your mother?"

Carrie slid the book into its proper slot while gathering her thoughts. She hadn't realized Mother's diagnosis was common knowledge, but in a town this small, she supposed word would get around eventually. Still, the conversation made her uncomfortable.

"As good as can be expected, I guess, given the situation." She checked the shelving numbers before turning to face the woman. Rhonda Flanders's face was too thin to wear long hair, but she wore it that way just the same, giving her a cartoonish appearance.

"Well," Rhonda said, oblivious to Carrie's

train of thought. "I, for one, thought, it was terrible the way they did her, after all the years she's put in."

Carrie reined in her musings about Rhonda's too-narrow face and tried to regroup, aware that she and Rhonda were not on the same page.

"I'm not sure what you mean, Rhonda. Who did something terrible to my mother?"

Rhonda's hand went to her lips. Her eyes widened. "You didn't know?"

Now Carrie was getting edgy. "Know what? Is my mother all right?"

"She's fine. At least, I suppose she is. I assumed she would have told you by now. It happened on Monday. Anyway, that's what Margaret Johnson told me and she was there when it happened."

Today was Thursday. "Rhonda, please. When *what* happened?"

"Well, I hate to be the bearer of bad news, but she is your mother and you have a right to know. The church board voted." Rhonda arranged her face in adequate sympathy. "They are replacing Frannie as church secretary effective immediately. She was fired."

July was hot enough without getting hot-under-the-collar to go along with the ninety-

227

degree temperatures. Carrie's fury gained momentum during the five-minute drive to her mother's house. How could they do this? After all Francis Adler had done for that church, years and years of self-sacrificing service and this was the thanks she got. Fired. *Fired.* The very word made Carrie so mad she could have chewed glass.

As she slammed out of her white Murano, she caught her purse strap in the door. Too upset to think straight, she jerked, snapping the strap in two.

Leaving the strip of tan leather dangling from the car, she hurried to Mother's front door.

Frannie's black-and-white cat, Tux, peered through the front window, mouth open in an unheard mew.

"Mother," Carrie called, opening the door without knocking. No answer. "Mother, are you home?"

The latter was a foolish question. Frannie's car sat beneath the detached fiberglass carport next to the house. Tux jumped down from his perch to wind through her legs. Carrie stood still for a moment, drawing in the cool rush of air-conditioning and listening for her mother's perky voice.

When none came, she started through the house with Tux underfoot. As she passed through the kitchen, she noticed something odd. Clothes and towels were strewn about, hanging over chair backs and on hangers hooked through cabinet pulls. Frannie was a relaxed housekeeper but not to this extent.

Tux meowed, a loud, complaining sound. He stood over an empty dish at the side of the refrigerator, yellow eyes staring up at her.

"What's wrong, Tux? No cat food?" She found the box and sprinkled a few fishy-smelling pebbles into the bowl before continuing the journey through the house.

She discovered her mother in the guest bedroom.

Bent over a dresser, Frannie was tossing clothes out with the vigor of a dog digging for a bone.

"Where is it?" she muttered.

"Mother? What are you doing?"

Frannie jumped, straightening so fast she bumped her elbow on a protruding drawer.

"Ouch. Oh fiddle." She shook her arm vigorously as she turned around. "Carrie Ann, you scared me, sneaking up like that."

"I've been calling your name for five minutes." Carrie looked around at the disaster in the bedroom. "What are you looking for?"

"That picture of Roland. Do you know

where it is? I think his phone number is on the back." She rubbed the tips of her fingers between her eyebrows. "Have you heard from him?"

Not only had Carrie not heard *from* him, she hadn't heard *of* him. "Who's Roland?"

Frannie stopped her frantic movements; a vague look crossed her face. She blinked rapidly and stared around the room.

"I always felt bad about hurting him that way. I thought he might have called." Suddenly, she plopped down on the bed amidst the mishmash of scarves and gloves and socks and other seldom-used items.

A quiver of uncertainty ran through Carrie. "Mother, I have no idea what you're talking about. Are you all right?"

Frannie's expression went blank. "I don't know. Wasn't Roland here?"

Carrie stood frozen to the spot, sickeningly afraid that her mother was having an episode that had nothing to do with reality. She didn't know what to do or say. Was it best to let Mother ramble? Or should she remind her of the here and now, bring her back into reality?

God, why don't You do something? This is hideous.

Silence pulsed in the room like some cruel beat of music until Tux found them. He hopped up onto the bed. Not caring that his owner was out of touch, the cat rubbed a whiskered jaw against Frannie's hand.

Struggling not to cry, Carrie slid down next to her mother and put an arm around her shoulders. "Mother, do you know me? Do you know where you are?"

For a moment, the only sounds were Tux's rumbling purr and the outside hum of someone's lawn mower. Carrie didn't know what to do but wait and hope that her mother would come back to reality.

As if the human and feline touches grounded her thinking, Frannie stroked the cat's head and spoke. "Of course I know who you are. Goodness' sakes, Carrie Ann. A mother knows her children."

Carrie breathed a sigh of relief but the tight pinch in her chest didn't go away.

"Who is Roland?"

"Roland." Voice caressing the word with an odd tenderness, Frannie stared down at the purring cat. Tux gazed back with a blink of gleaming yellow eyes. "Roland and I dated in high school, but then he went off to war and never came home."

"You never told me that. How did you hurt him?"

"Your daddy came along after Roland shipped out — older, more worldly — and swept me off my feet. I wrote Roland a Dear John letter." Her attention drifted across the room to a photo of her and Dad on their wedding day. Mother wore an enormous corsage on the shoulder of a Jackie Kennedy-style suit, her bouffant hair in a flip while the daddy she didn't remember looked smug in his skinny tie and button-down collar. "What a shameful thing to do to a soldier fighting for his country. I was a Christian girl. I knew better. Lord knows, I've repented of that many times."

"I'm sure the Lord has forgiven you." What else could she say?

"Oh, me, too. He's so sweet. He whispers in my heart that He doesn't remember my past sins, but I remember, and I'm still ashamed to have treated Roland that way. I've always wondered if my letter made him careless. They said he jumped out of a foxhole and charged up a hill under enemy fire. He won a Purple Heart and a Silver Star for saving his platoon. Not that he ever knew it."

"The war took him, Mother. Nothing in that was your fault."

"I hope not. I surely do. Roland James was a good boy who was sweet to everyone. And dance!" Frannie fanned herself. "You should have seen him do the Twist. Mercy!"

Carrie sat in utter amazement. She'd never thought of her mother as a teenager, much less a teenage heartbreaker.

"I don't know what made me think of him today," Frannie said, that lost look coming over her again.

"Me, either, Mother. But I'm glad you're okay."

"Right as rain." She didn't look right as rain. Her eyes were red-rimmed and tearstained and still a bit vague, but Carrie kept that to herself. "So what brings you here? Did I miss another dinner?"

"I heard something at the library. Something that upset me. What happened at the church?"

Her mother glanced away and then back again. Her shoulders drooped and, with a shock, Carrie thought she seemed suddenly, frighteningly old. "They let me go, honey. They had to. No need to be angry about it."

"Is that why you didn't tell me? Or did you —" She stopped short of asking the humiliating question.

"No, I didn't forget. You're already upset about this illness of mine. I didn't want to add to your worries."

Carrie sighed, deep and heavy, seething underneath. "You've worked for the church

233

in one capacity or another for years. Why did they do this to you?"

"See? I knew you'd take it all wrong." Frannie picked up the long, lanky cat and set him on her lap. "They had no choice. I can't do the work anymore, so I tendered my resignation."

Indignation rose as hot as steam. "Rhonda said they fired you." And they called themselves Christians.

"I guess they did. The mix-up in the speaker's dates was the last straw. All that airfare wasted." Mother slid a beringed hand over the cat, over his head and down his long, glossy back. A slight tremor shook her fingers as her face crumpled. "I don't want to forget, Carrie. I don't want to fade away like some old lady who has lost her mind."

The knowledge that this was exactly what would happen seared through Carrie. She closed her eyes against the look of agony on her mother's face.

God, she's served You faithfully. Where are You?

Where He always seemed to be when Carrie prayed — far away.

Frannie clawed at Carrie's hand, caught hold and squeezed hard. "Pray for a miracle, Carrie. We could get a miracle."

"Yes . . ." But Carrie didn't believe in miracles. "If anyone deserves one, you do."

Mother's grip went lax. Bewildered helplessness hovered in the room like an unwanted guest.

Carrie had no words to convey the sadness weighing beneath her breastbone. She simply didn't know what to do anymore. Her mother was a rock, a fortress of strength and determination. If Frannie lost control — which she eventually would — Carrie wasn't sure what would become of either of them.

Desperate for some way to escape her agonized thoughts, Carrie rose, the mattress groaning, and began to pick up the scattered items, folding and neatly replacing them in drawers.

After a few minutes, Frannie pushed Tux off her lap and rose from the patchwork-quilted bed to join Carrie in the cleanup effort.

"I made quite a mess, didn't I?" Her voice was quiet and regretful.

"Drawers need to be reorganized once in a while," Carrie said, as matter-of-factly as possible. With a snap of cloth, she shook out an outlandish fur blouse in leopard-skin print, then folded it next to an aqua leotard.

As Carrie smoothed the garments into

place, Fran placed a hand over hers, stopping her frantic busyness. "I'm sorry, honey. I didn't mean to let go like that. Sometimes I can't seem to help myself."

Carrie's eyes fell shut for one infinitesimal second. She didn't want to think about this. She didn't want to talk about it. But like an elephant in the room, the ugly facts filled the space and refused to be ignored.

She opened her eyes to the wide double mirror above the old dresser and looked at her mother. They shared the same chestnut-brown hair and wide forehead, but that's where the similarities ended. Now, a voice deep inside Carrie asked a frightening question. They were mother and child. Did Carrie, too, harbor the genetic disposition for Alzheimer's disease?

She spun away from the mirror and clutched at a handful of colorful scarves scattered on the floor in a kaleidoscope pattern. The smell of Mother's cologne rose from the silky material. How many times as a child had Carrie buried her face in Frannie's neck and inhaled that warm scent, secure in the knowledge that Mother would make everything all right.

Even in those difficult days of financial and emotional struggle after Jake Adler slipped off an oil derrick and tumbled to his death fifty feet below, leaving her with two toddlers and a funeral bill, Frannie had always taken good care of Carrie and Robby.

Now she'd lost her job. Soon she'd lose her mind.

Who would make things all right now?

CHAPTER FIVE

Carrie drove straight from Mother's house to the church. During the short drive, she formulated a dozen ways to get her point across, ending with the most powerful. She paid tithes to this church. Did they want to lose that?

Her conscience tweaked a bit, questioning if the threat of withholding finances was the proper way to handle the situation, but she refused to let the doubts stop her. This was her mother they were kicking around. Bunch of hypocrites. Carrie was defending someone in need. As long as the end justified the means, she wouldn't worry about the right or wrong of the action.

As she breezed into the outer office of Maple Street Congregation, she stopped short to discover Kathleen Filbert already ensconced at Mother's desk. Well, they certainly didn't let any grass grow under their feet.

"Hi, Carrie," Kathleen said, if a bit warily.

Ignoring the greeting, Carrie got straight to the point. "Is he in?"

"Reverend Ellis?"

"Yes." She was in no mood to call him Reverend. Anyone who would fire a dependable, enthusiastic, *sick* employee who worked as cheaply as Mother couldn't be too holy.

The door to the inner office opened and the gentle-faced minister stepped out. "Why, hello, Carrie. Did you need to see me?"

"I did." Hitching her chin an inch higher, she followed him inside and perched on the edge of a lovely upholstered armchair she'd likely paid for.

The minister settled behind the long, cherrywood desk. Above his head hung a picture of Jesus, hand outstretched, holding a rock. The caption said, "If any among you is without sin, let him cast the first stone."

Her thoughts exactly. They should have looked at their own problems before passing judgment on Mother. Not one of them was perfect, either.

Without preamble, she attacked. "My mother has worked for this church, with and without pay for as long as I can remember. And even if she hadn't, I would think a

Christian organization would have had more compassion for someone who was already struggling with the frightening diagnosis of Alzheimer's disease."

Reverend Ellis's mouth dropped. He blinked and leaned forward, forearms on the tidy desk. "Alzheimer's disease? I had no idea."

Carrie pulled back, equally stunned. "Mother didn't tell you?"

The man shook his head, an array of emotions moving through his pale blue eyes. "That explains so much, but no, Frannie didn't say one word about being ill."

Carrie put the finishing polish on a side table, complete with a vase of her very own lipstick snapdragons and blue bachelor's buttons. She was good with flower arrangements and loved the look of fresh flowers all through the house, but tonight her hands were simply going through the motions.

Dan had arrived home from work to collapse in his chair with the television blaring out bad news about war and death and the latest health scare. She had plenty of that already, thank you.

"Everything is falling apart, Dan," she said over the noise. "I don't know what to do."

Dan shifted in the chair. She could tell by

240

the incline of his head and the way his focus remained on the television that he was only half listening. "What's up?"

Besides the decibel level? "Two things. First, Mother had some kind of lapse today. One minute she was rambling about someone named Roland and the next she was back to normal."

Dan pointed the remote and pushed Mute. Now he was listening. The television meteorologist gestured at a U.S. map as if begging to be heard. "Your mother has never been normal."

"That's not funny anymore."

"And you're losing your sense of humor. Fran would have laughed."

Carrie huffed. Yes, Mother would have laughed, but nothing was funny.

She eyed the vase one last time, scooted it an inch to the left and decided that would have to do for now. She had more important business to worry about.

"The church fired her." She went to stand in front of him, one hand curled against her hip. "Three days ago, but she didn't tell us. She worried we'd be upset." A worry that was justified. Upset didn't begin to cover Carrie's feelings.

Two furrows appeared between Dan's eyebrows. He popped his recliner to a sitting position. "Fired her? Why?"

"Why do you think, Dan?" The man could be so obtuse. "She has Alzheimer's. She forgets things."

"A lot of patients are productive at work for a time, depending on their job and the progress of the disease." He grinned sheepishly; his wide shoulders bunched. "I've been reading on the Internet."

"Well, those sanctimonious church people who call themselves Christians didn't even bother to ask if anything was wrong, although the symptoms were there for all to see. Without an ounce of human compassion in their hearts, they threw Mother out like used mop water."

Dan's silence was telling. After trying to get him into church for years, this pretty much killed any chance of that happening. The man would never make Heaven at this rate. Well, it would be on the church's head. They could explain Dan's absence to God. Who would want to attend church with a bunch of hypocrites who preached Jesus's love and then kicked each other when the going got tough?

"Mother didn't say a word to defend herself. She let them fire her, gave them her blessing and cleaned out her desk. She never even mentioned the Alzheimer's diagnosis."

Dan ran a hand over the back of his neck, massaging a shoulder. "I'd say she handled it pretty well."

"She's devastated."

"Are you sure? Seems to me you're the one taking it so hard."

Carrie recoiled, stung. "I expected you to understand."

"I'm trying to, Carrie. This is hard on everyone."

She inhaled through her nose and exhaled in a huff. She wouldn't be a bit surprised to see steam flow out. "I don't know what to do."

"Nothing you can do." He reached for the newspaper and shook it open with a noisy crinkle. "If the church fired her, she's fired. Done deal."

"That's not what I meant. I'm talking about what to do with Mother."

"She's fine most of the time, Carrie. You said yourself, the spells come and go. You don't need to *do* anything with her." He bent his head to the paper. He was a master at hiding his head in the sand or, in this case, in the newspaper.

"Yet. But when? And how will we know?"

Without looking up, Dan said, "We'll know. Have you spoken to her doctor?"

"I called him as soon as I got home. He

doesn't seem particularly worried at this point," she admitted reluctantly. "He thinks Mother is coping quite well."

"There you are then."

Dan was so black-and-white at times he drove her insane. "What if she gets bad enough that we have to move her in with us?"

The paper crinkled again as he turned to the sports page. "We have plenty of room."

Exasperated, Carrie dropped her head back and stared at the ceiling. "It's not space that concerns me. Mother and I barely survived each other when I was a teenager. I can't live with her."

"Would you stop borrowing trouble and just fix dinner? My ham sandwich wore off about an hour ago."

Carrie threw her hands into the air. "I should have known your stomach was more important than my mother."

With a sigh, Dan laid aside the newspaper and headed to the refrigerator. "Never mind. I'll grill."

Guilt crept in like an unwanted guest. "I was going to make meat loaf."

Dan paid her no mind. Head stuck inside the freezer, he asked in a muffled voice, "Should I thaw out a steak for Lexi?"

"She's spending the night at Courtney's."

Which meant she wouldn't be here to act as a buffer in the cold war brewing between her parents. Carrie and Dan never fought in front of Lexi. Ever. As far as their daughter knew, they had the perfect marriage. They did most of the time. But sometimes during a crisis, Carrie felt as she had during those childbearing years when month after month had passed and she'd not been able to conceive. Alone. Let down. A failure.

"You put on the steaks. I'll make those double-baked potatoes you like so much." His favorite food was the best truce she knew how to offer.

Package of frozen steaks in one hand and the other holding the freezer door open, Dan turned to look at her, some of the stiffness leaving his sturdy shoulders. She wanted him to comfort her, to tell her everything would be all right.

Instead, he said, "Fine," slammed the freezer and went to the microwave. The cold scent of refrigerated air wafted out and mingled with the scent of tea steeping on the stove. The combination made her stomach roll.

She went to the pantry for potatoes, dejection pressing in like an ominous black cloud.

Frannie had been looking for an opportunity

to talk to Dan alone for three days. When none presented itself, she did what she'd always done. She took the bull by the horns and called him up, asking him to stop by on his way home from the gym.

Now, he sat in her living room, drinking Mountain Dew and pretending to admire her latest hat. He was the sweetest thing. She had thanked God a thousand times for sending Dan Martin into her daughter's life.

"I didn't really ask you over here to look at my hat." She set the pale pink confection on the coffee table.

"I figured as much. What's up? A snake in the bushes?" He reached down to scratch Tux's ears. The old tom purred loudly.

She laughed. "I hope not. Carrie about had apoplexy over the last one." She took a sip of her own soda pop, letting the fizz bubble in her throat. "I'm running out of time, Dan."

He set his glass on the table, expression growing serious. "You seem fine to me."

"Most of the time. But we both know I won't be for long, so let's move on past that. I need your help."

"Anything."

"Carrie."

Broad hands on his jean-clad thighs, he nodded slowly. "I'm concerned, too. She stays worked up all the time like she's mad at me and I don't know what I've done wrong."

"It's not you, Danny boy." The statement seemed to relieve him. "Carrie's been upset for a long time."

"I think you're right, but she's worse lately. I love her more than anything, but I don't know what to say to her anymore."

Fran patted his arm. "She thinks she let you down. Do you know that?"

Two furrows creased the space between his eyebrows. "No way. How?"

"Babies."

"Oh."

"I think it was the babies that turned her bitter."

"You think that's the problem? After all this time?"

"I think she blames God for letting her down. For letting you down."

He rubbed his chin, a scratchy, masculine sound. Tux hopped up to smell his face. "I get what you're saying. Carrie thinks God is letting everyone down again because of you. She's mad at God."

Frannie nodded. "Right. Carrie has this notion that if we work hard enough, do enough for God, He should make our lives perfect."

Dan smiled, if a little sadly. "Carrie does like for everything to be perfect."

"Yes, she does. Perfect house. Perfect flowers. Even her hair has to be cut exactly right or she's in a huff for a week. But life isn't perfect and God never said we wouldn't have heartache and trouble."

"I still don't know what to do."

Hoping to lighten him up and make him laugh, Frannie clapped her hands and rubbed them together like the villain in a movie. "Then you've come to the right place. Grannie Frannie has a few ideas."

Dan's smile was a start. "I was afraid you'd say that."

It was Fran's turn to smile. "First, I need a promise."

"You got it."

"When my time comes, when I become a burden and get lost and can't take care of myself, make Carrie put me in Sunset Care Center. I've already checked out the facilities, the care, the staff. It's a good place."

The smile went out of him faster than a flea hop. "Fran."

"Promise me, Dan."

He shook his head. "I don't know if I can."

"You said you'd do anything. I need to know I won't be a burden on my loved ones. That's the thing that scares me most. I can

248

handle fading into the sunset. I can't handle knowing I've shortchanged all of you."

Dan picked up his soft drink and sipped; his Adam's apple bobbed, a reminder of the last time she'd talked to Ken. Funny how her mind could forget some things and cling to others that she'd like to forget.

"Please, Dan. I need this."

He set the glass down again. "All right, Frannie. For you and for Carrie, I'll see to it."

She let out a breath she hadn't realized she was holding. "Thank you, Danny. I love you, you know."

"I know." He gulped again, his eyes growing dangerously moist. For a man like Dan, showing this much emotion must be killing him.

"Carrie needs you to love her unconditionally right now, Dan. Even when she's a pain in the neck, and Lord knows she can be a big one, love her."

"I do."

"No, I mean, hold her, touch her, talk to her, let her know you're sharing her pain."

"She's been pretty distant lately."

"Then double up. Be sweet and huggy-kissy-lovey. She needs you to do that for her."

Dan shook his head, a soft smile lifting

the corners of his mouth. "You're something, Frannie."

"No, honey, the Lord is something. Without Him I got no strength at all. Which brings me to the last thing I want to talk to you about."

"I can see there's no escape."

Fran giggled. "None at all, my boy, so take it like a man."

He pretended to brace himself.

"You might think about going to church with Carrie. Having you there would mean a lot to her."

He bristled. "I may not attend church, Frannie, but I believe in Jesus. Carrie has trouble understanding that, but I do."

"I know you do, honey. Your faith is obvious to anyone who looks. I believe a real Christian will be known by two things: By his love for others and the good fruit he bears. You aced the test a long time ago. But your wife puts a lot of stock in appearances. She'd love to have you sitting in a pew on Sunday morning."

Dan's jaw tensed. "I can't stomach being in a church with Jeff Rogers on the board when I know he cheats on his wife and knocks her around."

Fran had suspected as much. "That's an ugly thing, Danny boy, and Jeff will answer

250

for his actions, but he has nothing to do with *your* relationship with God."

He chewed on that for a few seconds. "I'll think about it."

Frannie was satisfied with that. It was a start.

"One last thing."

Dan's mouth twitched. "Hit me with it."

"About those children the two of you always wanted? Well, The Lord and I have a brilliant idea." She winked. "But I'm going to need your cooperation."

Praying he would agree, Fran launched into an explanation of her plan.

CHAPTER SIX

By the time the heat of August sucked the breath from the lungs and caused the grass to shrivel into brown, crispy straws, Carrie had stopped trying to pray because it was pretty obvious God wasn't listening. If she was honest, she was still upset with the church, even though they'd been unaware of Frannie's illness. She continued to attend Sunday-morning service and to serve on committees, but a coldness had settled into her spirit that she couldn't seem to shake. Worship service and church work left her drained instead of inspired.

A bead of sweat rolled between Carrie's shoulder blades. She lifted the hair off the back of her neck.

"I hate August," she said to Lexi as they crossed Frannie's yard. Though Mother still attended her clubs, visited friends and flitted about town like a woman without a care, Carrie made a point of stopping by every day to see how things were going.

Some days were good. Some not so good. Like the proverbial box of chocolates, she never knew what she'd get. Today, the trio had a shopping date. For Lexi's sake, Carrie hoped Grannie Frannie remembered.

The bright green front door swung open with a reverberating bang. "There's my girls! Come in, come in. I made a blackberry cobbler. Picked the blackberries myself from Blantons' garden." She hitched her shoulders in a girlish shrug. "With their permission, of course."

"Yum. Is there ice cream?" Lexi stopped in the doorway for a hug before going inside, nose sniffing the pie-scented interior.

"Can't have pie without ice cream." Frannie wrapped Carrie in a fluffy embrace. For an infinitesimal beat of time, Carrie let herself forget Mother's illness long enough to absorb the love like a dry sponge absorbs liquid.

"You smell like Avon cobbler," Carrie teased against Frannie's soft hair.

Her mother laughed and pulled away. "I guess I invented a new fragrance. You want pie before or after shopping?"

"Better ask Lex. She's the one who's always starving."

"Skinny little thing." Frannie patted her

wide hips. "Takes after her granny."

Relieved to know that today was a good day, Carrie smiled along with her mother as they trailed into the house. Lexi came out of the kitchen, a giant spoon of steaming cobbler in one hand, the other cupped below in case of drips.

"Just a bite before we leave, okay?" Without waiting for a reply, she nibbled the edges of the spoon and made a humming sound. "Grannie Frannie makes the best cobbler in Oklahoma. Maybe even in America."

"No argument from me," Carrie said. "Or anyone in Riverbend." Her mother's home-made pies had funded more than one mission trip. "We'll pig out when we get back."

"What's our modus operandi today?" Frannie asked. From the back of the couch, she took out a bright red hat trimmed with a tall flowerlike spray of royal blue sequins and fitted it over her neatly coiffed bob. Around her neck she wound a gauzy, multi-colored scarf in shades of blue and red and yellow. "How do I look?"

"Smashing," Carrie lied, much preferring her navy slacks and linen blouse to Mother's sparkly slides and wild hats. "Fit for the Kentucky Derby."

"I always wanted to attend the Derby,"

Mother said. "All those wonderful hats . . . Now that I don't have a job to stop me, maybe next year I'll just get up and go."

Carrie kept her opinion to herself, though regret pinched her like cheap shoes. Mother loved travel and adventure, and she'd had little time or money for either. Now, no one, especially Frannie, knew what her state of mind would be next week, much less months in the future.

"Do you think this is too low cut?" Lexi came out of the dressing room at a trendy teen boutique wearing an adorable smocked top with a plunging V-neck. She tugged at the shoulders.

Carrie held up a baby doll top in pastel plaid. Shopping for modest school clothes that were still trendy and acceptable to a teenager became harder with each passing year. "How about this top with a pair of leggings?"

Lexi tilted her head and squinted. "Cute. Let me try it."

Frannie grabbed the leggings from a rack and handed them off. Lexi disappeared behind the dressing room door. "Disaster averted."

"She knew the top was too low," Carrie said, sorting through a rack of outlandishly

255

priced blue jeans. "Asking was a test to see if I'd get hysterical."

"You passed." Frannie picked up a Scottish plaid beret with a silver buckle. "Oh, this is darling."

"Lexi's not much for hats, except her softball cap."

"Not for Lexi. For me! Here, hold my hat while I try it."

With a chuckle, Carrie took the red hat and watched as her mother preened in front of the mirror. Lexi stepped out of the dressing booth, fresh and young and adorable in the top and leggings.

"Gran, you look amazing."

"You, too, rosebud. Think I can catch a beau in this beret?"

"Are we talking about Mr. Markovich?"

One hand adjusting the plaid beret, Mother paused. A shadow passed over her face, and Carrie had a frightening thought that she was going into one of her spells.

"Oh, he's old news."

Carrie relaxed a tiny bit but kept her attention on Frannie. Though not a forgetting spell, something had disturbed her mother. Carrie found herself remembering an odd incident from church last Sunday. The three of them had passed Ken Markovich as they'd entered the foyer. Mother had hesitated for a moment, her vermilion smile faltering as she greeted the man who'd been her companion for a long time. Instead of their usual round of silly teasing, followed by an invitation to sit with him, both had looked acutely uncomfortable. When she'd ask Frannie later if they were sitting together, her mother had simply said, "Not today."

Now she wondered what was going on.

But if Frannie was troubled by Lexi's teasing, she recovered well. She bumped her granddaughter with a hip. "What about you and that Fielding boy? Hmm?"

Lexi giggled and hitched both shoulders. "I'll never tell."

Frannie widened her eyes and acted silly as she scooted up next to Lexi in front of the long mirror.

"Gorgeous, Lex, my rosebud."

"Gorgeous, Grannie Frannie."

The pair stood chattering and studying themselves as they'd done a hundred times before on shopping trips. Pretending to look through an assortment of purses, Carrie listened to the conversation and relaxed. Today was a good day. No use borrowing trouble about Ken Markovich.

Lexi went back inside the dressing booth to change clothes and Mother wandered off to peruse the jewelry racks. She'd probably return with enough fake gold to impress the ancient Aztecs.

"What did you decide?" Carrie asked when Lexi reappeared, clothes draped over her arm.

"I like these. But I really want some new jeans, too. Can I have both?"

"I'm not paying a hundred dollars for a pair of jeans."

Lexi huffed in exasperation. "Next summer I'm getting a job."

"Great idea." Carrie leaned her forehead against Lexi's and whispered. "But for this year, you'll have to settle for ordinary jeans at ordinary prices."

Though clearly believing her mother was the most uncool, stingiest mom on the planet, Lexi got over being miffed in a hurry.

"Murielle's has cute stuff cheap," she said, mentioning a shop on the opposite end of the mall.

"Sounds like a plan. Let's tell your grandmother."

Lexi's thick-lashed eyes, gray-blue like her father's, made a quick survey of the crowded store. "Where is Grannie Frannie?"

Carrie glanced around and pointed in the general direction her mother had gone. "She was over by the accessories."

"Buying boas?" Lexi asked, grinning.

"You do know your Grannie." Carrie slung an arm across her daughter's slender shoulders. "Come on. Let's find her and go before she buys another ugly hat."

"There she is, Mom." Lexi waved.

Standing near the back wall, Frannie gazed out at the store with a worried expression. Carrie waved, too, but got no response. Her pulse accelerated. Didn't Mother see them?

She picked up her pace until she reached her mother's side. "Mother?"

Frannie clutched her arm. "Carrie, I want to go home."

"But we just got here."

"I can't take this noise. It's making me too confused. I can't breathe. I need to go home." Frannie took off, heading out the boutique door and into the mall.

Exchanging a look of puzzled dismay, Lexi and Carrie rushed after her.

An hour later, over cobbler and ice cream, Frannie apologized for the abrupt departure. "I don't know what came over me. The noise in that place made my head swim. I thought I was going to have a panic attack."

"You've always loved shopping."

"I'll be better tomorrow. We can try

again." She patted Lexi's arm. "You didn't have a chance to buy that cute outfit, did you?"

"No big deal." Lexi stirred her spoon around in the melting ice cream, not making eye contact. This was the first time she had witnessed one of her grandmother's episodes of confusion. Carrie's heart ached for her. She and Frannie had always been like two peas in a pod.

Carrie pushed off the bar stool and took her dirty bowl to the dishwasher. To tell the truth, she hadn't enjoyed the much-anticipated cobbler at all. Though as tasty as always, it stuck in her throat.

"Mother, are you finished with yours?"

Frannie handed over the dish and said, "I'm really tired. I think I'll lie down for a while."

Mother's energy was boundless. She'd never been known to nap.

"All right. I'll straighten the kitchen and we'll head home. Mind if I take Dan a dish of cobbler?"

Frannie waved a listless hand. "Sure, sure. Take whatever you want." As she started out of the kitchen, she stopped, turned and said, "I'm sorry about our shopping trip. I feel so stupid now."

■ ■ ■ ■

Carrie and Lexi were quiet in the car, both of them reflective, though Lexi's CD provided the right amount of cover noise. Carrie had never fussed about her daughter's choice of music, partly because she and Fran had fought like billy goats over Carrie's teenage admiration for Madonna. Frannie tended toward flamboyance. Why should she object to an entertainer who did the same thing? Carrie hadn't understood for the longest time. Now she did, of course, but she'd vowed to be more rational and accepting with her own children. As long as the lyrics were appropriate, the scratchy guitars or bumping bass didn't bother her in the least. Today the heavy thump of the music pounding from the speakers reflected the heaviness in her heart.

"Mom?" Lexi said after a bit, leaning forward to turn down the radio.

Carrie's hands tightened on the steering wheel. "What, hon?"

"Is Grannie Frannie going to get worse?"

Her heart thudded once, hard. "Only God knows the answer to that, but if she follows the usual course, yes, she'll get worse."

"What causes Alzheimer's?"

"No one really knows for certain. Something in the brain goes awry."

"There's no cure?" The ache in her daughter's tone echoed the one inside Carrie's chest.

"No, not yet."

"I don't want to lose her, Mom. I'm going to pray that they find a cure in time to make Grannie well."

"You do that, sweetheart." No point in destroying Lexi's faith, just because her own was at an all-time low.

"Is Alzheimer's disease hereditary?"

Carrie's stomach dipped. She hadn't been expecting that question, had intentionally avoided thinking in that vein. "I think something genetic may be involved, yes."

A contemplative silence hovered as they slowed for a traffic light. Cars with the right-of-way chugged through the intersection emitting the hum of single-lane traffic.

When the light beamed green and Carrie pressed her foot to the accelerator, Lexi said, "Mom?"

She flicked a glance toward her daughter. Lexi's slim, suntanned fingers fidgeted with a plastic CD case.

"What?"

"When you get old, will Alzheimer's happen to you, too?"

Dear God, she hoped it would not. But how could she tell her daughter no? The only answer was the truth.

"I don't know, Lexi. No one knows."

Her whole body ached to think that her beloved only child might have to walk in her shoes. Lexi may someday have to face the hard lessons Carrie was only beginning to learn. Worst of all she may have to watch helplessly as her mother changed and ultimately disappeared, little by little.

The knowledge frightened Carrie to the point of asking herself a terrible question. If she knew Alzheimer's was happening to her, would she be tempted to do something final and drastic to spare her precious child this agony? And if she did, would she be forever condemned?

No answer came, of course. And that was the deepest agony of all. The darkness that lingered constantly in the back of her mind pushed to the fore. Where was God when she needed Him so badly?

CHAPTER SEVEN

Bright and early Saturday morning, before the neighbors fired up the lawn mowers and while neighborhood dogs raced through flower beds to do their business, Frannie marched through Carrie's front door. Wearing camouflage knickers and a T-shirt beneath a beige safari hat, she whipped off her aviator sunglasses. "Where's Dan?"

Carrie, still poring over the morning paper and nursing a second cup of freshly perked coffee, didn't bat an eye. Mother's unpredictable nature had existed long before Alzheimer's disease entered the picture. Seeing her like this was actually a good sign.

She motioned toward the kitchen exit. "Out in the garage. He and Lexi are bonding over that old Camaro."

Without further ado, Mother sailed past like a soldier in hot pursuit, out into the garage.

Curious, Carrie put down the paper, took

her coffee and followed. What in the world was Mother up to this morning?

The garage was stuffy, though Dan had opened the huge outer door to let in light and a draft of fresh air. Carrie left the kitchen door open and sat down on the single step, air-conditioning at her back. If she was going to work in her flowers this morning, she needed to get with it before the heat took over.

Directly in front of her, Dan and Lexi had their heads together beneath the hood of a metallic-blue Camaro, Dan's first car — a car he'd preserved for the son they'd planned to have. He and his boy would rebuild and restore the car together, a father-son activity that would bond them through the rough teenage years. Carrie knew this plan, of course, though Lexi had no idea.

Years ago, Dan had quietly changed the plan. Without fanfare or a rehash of his broken dream, he'd relegated the classic car to his daughter. The two of them would restore the Camaro and on her sixteenth birthday, the car would belong to her. To everyone's surprise, particularly Lexi's, she enjoyed working on the Camaro with her dad. For Carrie, the car bond offered a sense of absolution.

She heard Dan's deep rumble as he talked to his daughter. She loved Dan's voice, a sound as strong and masculine as the man. He was a man's man, the kind of guy who could fix a car or a busted water line, work all day in the heat or cold or rain and never flinch. But mention a wedding or a trip to the mall and he got that haunted, deer-in-headlights look and retreated to the garage or a fishing pond somewhere. Carrie's lips curved on the edge of her coffee mug. Dan.

By this time, Frannie had reached the fender of the Camaro. Tilting her head to look beneath the hood, she said, "Danny boy, I need your help."

The rumble of Dan's voice ceased.

From her vantage point, Carrie saw his wide, grease-smudged hand reach for a red mechanic's rag before his head appeared. Lexi popped up beside him.

"Hi, Grannie Frannie. Want to help us change spark plugs?" The end of her nose was tipped in grease.

"I wouldn't know a spark plug from a fireplug. But I know a shopping bag. That outfit you tried on the other day is out in my car. Jeremy Fielding won't know what hit him."

Over Dan's scowl at the mention of his daughter's latest beau, Lexi cried, "Gran!

You are the best."

"And don't you ever forget it," Frannie said, shaking a finger. "Even if I do." While everyone else grappled to see the humor in her bad joke, Frannie turned her focus on Dan. "I have a proposition for you, Dan the man."

Slowly wiping his hands on the red rag, Dan said, "Should I be nervous?"

"Absolutely." Like a comic with perfect timing, she widened her eyes and waited a split second while her jest soaked in. She and Dan had always had this easy banter between them.

"What are you going to try to talk me into?" Humor crinkled the corners of his eyes.

"We're having a cookout for the Children's Church kids at Dale Patrosky's farm, complete with fishing, horseback riding, and enough hot dogs and cookies to make them all sick. I volunteered for the fishing."

After losing her job at the church, Mother hadn't missed a beat. While Carrie stewed and fumed, Mother went right on volunteering, working on committees, baking cookies and helping with any and everything the church needed. Carrie didn't get the point. Why bother if neither God nor man appreciated the effort?

She started up from the step. "By your-self?"

"Good gravy, no. Even I wouldn't tackle that many kids alone. That's where Dan comes in." She aimed this last remark at her son-in-law. "It's a crying shame, but we never have enough men. Half these kids come to church with only a mother and the other half come on the bus without any parent at all. Poor little lambs. No wonder society is in such a mess. No male role models."

Dan used the tip of the rag to polish a spot on his thumbnail. "I feel a guilt trip coming on."

Frannie laughed and patted his shoulder. "That's because I'm orchestrating one. Tell me this, Daniel Martin, how is a boy supposed to learn to be a man if he's always around a bunch of us old hens?"

"You got me there."

"Good. I knew I could count on you. Thursday evening at five-thirty. You'll have the time of your life."

"And all the hot dogs I can eat?"

"Absolutely."

"I'll help, too, Grannie," Lexi said. "As long as I don't have to touch a worm."

In a conspiratorial stage whisper, Frannie said, "That's why we need your dad."

268

Dan tossed the red cloth toward a tool-box. "I heard that."

The three of them grinned at each other like baboons while Carrie listened in amazement. She had tried for years to get Dan involved in church activities. Then Mother waltzes in, talks about boys and fishing, and he gives in without so much as an argument.

Patroskys' farm was little more than a horse corral, a pond and a stand of woods, but it was the perfect place for a bunch of rowdy town kids to learn about outdoor recreation in a positive environment. Mother flitted up and down the pond edge, her bawdy laugh echoing over the water in conjunction with the squeals and chatter of thirty or more kids.

Carrie wasn't sure how she'd gotten roped into the outing, considering the resentment she felt toward most of the adult attendees. But she'd been so intrigued at Dan's enthusiastic involvement she hadn't wanted to be left out.

"Come on, Mom." Lexi gestured from her spot next to Dan along the grassy bank. "I saved a lawn chair for you."

"Did you use bug spray?" Wielding a can of Off! Carrie moved from the shady cook-out area toward the pond.

"Yes, Mom."

"Spray these other kids, Carrie," her mother called.

Most of the town kids wore shorts and flip-flops, a poor choice for horseback riding and traipsing through knee-high pastures. She doubted if any of them had used sunscreen or Off! before boarding the church van.

"Line up, kids, if you want bug spray." Children of all sizes and shapes came running as if she were handing out free Nintendo games, arms out to their sides, while she fanned the insecticide around their bodies. Carrie turned her head away from the strong odor. "Any bug brave enough to come through this stuff deserves the free meal."

When the last child was sprayed, Carrie stood alone, can in hand, wondering what to do now. She wasn't much for fishing, though she supposed her knowledge was more than most of these kids. And she certainly didn't want to sit in the circle of lawn chairs around the campfire with the other adults from the church, making small talk. She had nothing to say to those people anymore. It was hard to be chatty with resentment churning inside her.

At a loss, she finally journeyed down the

embankment toward Dan to help with the fishing. A gaggle of children surrounded her husband, touching him, talking to him, soaking up every word he said. From his expression, Dan loved every moment of it. He was born to be a daddy, a truth never clearer than today.

Beside her, a little girl with honey-blond hair and smooth, tanned skin reeled in an empty line.

"Your worm is gone, Bailey." Carrie pointed to the empty hook.

"Can you put a new one on for me?"

Carrie cringed and looked toward Dan, who was too busy to notice. "Uh, sure."

Bracing herself, she dug in the dirt-filled container for a wiggly night crawler and threaded it onto the hook.

"Stinks, don't it?" Bailey asked, watching every move of Carrie's now-filthy fingers.

"Sure does. But the fish love them. Have you caught one yet?"

"No. But I asked Jesus to let me get one. He knew all about fishing. Rev. Ellis said He was a fisher of men. But I think he was joking. Men don't live in ponds and eat worms."

While Carrie absorbed that bit of adorable wisdom, a shout went up. "I got one. I got one."

Dan dropped a plastic sack of bobbers and raced toward the young fisherman, a solemn-eyed boy with mocha skin and curly hair. "Pull him in, son. Nice and easy. That's it. You got him. Here he comes."

The boy reeled desperately, his wide, dark eyes flashing from the bent line to Dan's face and back again. He pushed the reel toward Dan. "You do it. I can't."

Dan remained beside the boy but refused to take the reel. "Yes, you can. You've almost got him. Don't give up. This one's yours, buddy."

As if he'd needed that bit of encouragement, the youngster set his feet in the soft, moist earth and reeled harder. By now, half a dozen other children had come running, offering words of advice and yells of excitement.

Dan leaned forward, ready to grab the line the moment the fish broke above the water. "Here he comes. He's a good one."

As the bass surfaced, the noise around the pond increased. The fisherman sent up a shout of jubilee. "I got him. I got him. He's huge."

The now-banked fish flopped and twisted, scales glistening in the evening sun. Dan clapped the boy on the back. "I knew you could do it."

The boy looked up at him and finally let his smile come. It spread over his face, into his dark eyes and finally out to his body. A gurgle of laughter, pure and delightful, erupted.

Carrie smiled and headed that direction as Dan showed all the gathered kids the proper way to remove the hook.

"Anyone have a camera before we release Shamu back into the wild?" Dan asked, urging the grinning boy to hold the bass aloft for all to admire.

"I'm coming." Digital camera glinting silver in the sun, Frannie untangled herself from a circle of kids playing blindman's bluff and trotted over.

Once the photo was taken, Dan and the boy squatted side by side to release the fish back into the water. Carrie watched them, a hitch beneath her ribs, as the boy looked up at Dan with an expression of hero worship. Such a simple thing to help a boy catch a fish and yet both males glowed with pleasure.

By the end of the evening, when the sun began to fade and the children loaded the church bus to return home, Carrie sat in a lawn chair with Dan at her side, tired but feeling positive. Her mother had been as exuberant as ever, without a hint of the dementia, and Dan had had a wonderful time.

"You were great with those kids, Dan," she murmured, rolling her head to look at his profile. "B.J. stuck to you like a wood tick."

He returned her gaze. "He doesn't have a dad in his life."

She knew. "Sad."

"Not a bad kid."

"Yet."

"Yeah. I was thinking maybe I'd spend some time with him. Teach him some boy things. Him and a couple of the others were asking if they could come over to the house sometime."

"And you said yes."

"You don't mind, do you?"

Ten-year-old boys running through her house and flowers. As if she didn't have enough problems dealing with Mother.

But hadn't she wished for more children in the house? Hadn't she prayed for God to send Dan a little boy?

Thinking that God had a warped sense of timing, she only said, "No, I don't mind."

In the days following the cookout, Dan and B.J. struck up a friendship that had the fatherless street kid hanging out at the Martin house more than at home. Both males seemed to thrive on the relationship, and any annoyance Carrie felt at having dirt tracked on her clean tile was offset by watching a somber boy begin to blossom.

Most times, Carrie managed not to think about her mother's illness too much, though she couldn't get past her annoyance at people. First the church had betrayed Mother and now Ken, for she was certain he had. The old coot. After years of squiring Mother around, he'd disappeared like the hot dogs at the cookout.

Frannie, in her inimitable style, went right on as if nothing had happened. She laughed, she clogged, she played her guitar and watched the skydiving. The day after the cookout, she and Alice had signed up for a karate class.

She was forgetting more. Carrie could see it so clearly now, though the occasional episodes of confusion were the worst. Even Alice mentioned them. So, if Mother forgot to pay her electric bill on time or put the iron in the refrigerator, Carrie simply paid the bill or moved the iron without comment.

But thinking about Mother's decline drove her to despair.

On a quiet Wednesday when the wind was hot and unwelcome and everyone prayed for a rain that didn't come, Carrie bought a basket of rich-scented peaches from a farmer in the parking lot of Ace Hardware.

Today was Mother's Red Hat Society meeting. Carrie didn't worry about her when she was with the girls, all of whom knew her diagnosis.

Once she'd reached the house and put away the groceries, she dug out the ice-cream maker. Homemade peach ice cream, Dan's favorite, would hit the spot on this hot, dry day. Maybe she'd marinate some pork chops and grill some corn on the cob, as well. She'd throw on extra in case B.J. and his buddies showed up.

As she organized the ingredients and chopped peaches, she hummed a happy tune and now and then snitched a bite of the juicy fruit. Life seemed better today, as if she had faced a trial and adjusted.

When the phone rang, she wiped her hands on a dish towel and reached for the receiver. "Hello."

"Carrie?"

She didn't recognize the voice. "Yes?"

"This is Claudia Davis." The woman who lived across the street from Mother.

"Oh, hi, Claudia. How are you?" Cradling the phone between her shoulder and ear, she reached for another peach.

276

"Honey, do you know where your mother is?"

Something in Claudia's voice sounded odd. Carrie placed the peach on the counter.

"At the Red Hat Society." She glanced at the clock on the microwave. "Or she may be home by now. Why?"

"Carrie, I hate to tell you this, but Frannie's house is on fire."

CHAPTER EIGHT

Sirens pierced the hot, breezy afternoon like screams. Carrie's legs shook as she parked her car a block from Mother's and took off in a dead run toward the flashing, whirling emergency lights. Her purse flapped against her side. Why she'd stopped to get her purse was a mystery she had no time to solve.

Both sides of the quiet two-lane street were packed with cars and emergency vehicles. Uniformed emergency workers swarmed the neighborhood like ants at a picnic.

A wall of yellow-coated firefighters rimmed the perimeter of Mother's house spilling out into the street to a long, red ladder truck. One firefighter stood atop the truck working gauges while others pulled a huge beige hose toward the flaming structure.

With a sick jolt, Carrie realized they were too late to save Mother's little frame house.

Their focus was on keeping the fire contained and protecting the surrounding structures.

"Oh no, not this, too."

Stricken, she slowed her pace, searching through the clusters of neighbors and nosy disaster chasers for a short, squat woman in a big red hat.

"Has anyone seen Frannie Adler?" she called toward one of the groups. They parted like the Red Sea, staring at her with interest and curiosity. Some of the people she knew. Others were strangers. Nosy strangers who'd come to watch her mother's house burn in both sympathy for the victim and gratitude that the disaster hadn't happened to them.

In a small town like Riverbend, people took their excitement where they could, and a house fire was big news.

"Carrie, honey." Mother's next-door neighbor, Sara Cummings, rushed forward and hugged her. The gray-haired woman had been Carrie's high school math teacher. "I don't think your mother was home."

Heart thudding painfully against her ribs, Carrie nodded, trying to calm the panic and distress flooding through her veins like the water from those fire hoses. "She was supposed to be at the Red Hat Society."

"Thank the good Lord."

"But I can't find her. I thought she'd be home by now." The wind blew her hair into a swirling mess. A strand slapped across her mouth. She reached up and pulled it away, knowing that her hair, like the fire, was out of control in this kind of wind. Mother's house hadn't stood a chance.

"I was just about to start supper." Sara gazed at the soaring flames as she spoke. "I went out in the garden to cut a mess of okra. Bob isn't supposed to eat fried foods, but he loves okra." She smiled softly. "You know how it is. First thing I noticed when I opened the back door was the smoke. Whew, it burned my eyes something fierce. Right then, I knew a fire was awful close."

"Were you the one who called the fire department?"

"Yes, but I guess someone else already had because dispatch said they were on the way." She turned toward her one-story brick. A hummingbird feeder strung from the porch rafters swung in the stiff breeze. "Bob's gathering up our important papers in case the fire gets to us."

"Oh, I hope not, Sara. Is it safe for him to be in there?"

"A fireman went over with him. Told him to make it fast."

Carrie had to agree. "Thank you for calling 9-1-1. You've been a good neighbor to Mother."

Sara patted her arm. "Frannie is a good neighbor to all of us."

"I have to find her. She's going to be devastated."

"Who wouldn't be? Let me know if I can do anything. Tell Frannie I said that."

With barely a nod, Carrie rushed off to speak to a firefighter wearing a red captain's helmet. Before she could reach him, a car horn blared long and loud. Carrie whirled toward the familiar sound, heart leaping into her throat. The street was cordoned off, but half a block away The Tanker slammed to a halt next to a birdbath on Jack Rodell's front lawn, and Mother leaped out.

The surge of relief at seeing her mother alive and well was an adrenaline high like no other. Hurdling a hodgepodge of unfamiliar-looking equipment, Carrie dipped and darted between parked cars and around emergency vehicles in an effort to touch Frannie, to assure herself that Frannie was truly safe.

"Mother!" she cried, running full steam ahead.

They met in the middle of Oak Street in the narrow space between an SUV and an empty police car. Trembling like a leaf, Mother fell against Carrie. Throughout her life, Carrie had been held in Frannie's arms many times as Mother soothed and prayed away her daughter's hurts. Today, the roles were reversed, as Carrie feared they would be in the months and years to come. With the stench of smoke in her nostrils and the heat of summer like a weight, she gathered her mother close and held tight.

Mother's face was stark white behind bright red lipstick and aviator sunglasses. Her breath came in short pants. "What happened? My house. My house."

"It's gone." The cruel words scraped across her tongue.

Frannie slowly peeled off the sunglasses and stared in wide-eyed horror at the scene playing out in her front yard. "Everything? All of it?"

Carrie nodded, sick at her stomach to be the conveyor of such news.

As Frannie gazed toward the only home she'd ever owned, her face drooped like melted candle wax.

"Did they save anything? Anything at all?" Her mother's voice contained such pain, Carrie could only shake her head and fight back tears. The fire was one more in a long list of last straws. How much more could

Mother take before she broke completely?

With the strength that had carried her through a lifetime of ups and downs, Frannie squared her shoulders and hitched her Hawaiian print tote bag. "I need to see for myself."

Heavy smoke and bits of ash floated on the wind. Ashes of Mother's life. The gray ghost of a refrigerator poked up through the piles of glowing, charred, unrecognizable objects. One final, tenacious wall crumbled beneath the force of a fire hose.

As they drew as close as firefighters would allow, neighbors formed a semicircle around them. Some just stood there at a loss for words. Others offered murmurs of sympathy, while others speculated on the cause of the fire.

"Old house like that is a tinderbox."

Carrie gave the hook-nosed speaker a hard glare. He dropped his gaze and hushed. Silly old thing. Didn't he have any common sense?

Mother, usually a wealth of conversation, stood in dejected silence, her hat knocked askew, one snazzy red shoe missing.

It occurred to Carrie then that the only clothes Mother owned were on her back. They'd have to find that shoe.

"A crying shame, Frannie." Sara Cummings had walked over to pat Frannie's back.

Frannie, her stricken gaze on the destroyed home, suddenly clutched Carrie's arm in a death grip. Her hands were hot and clammy. "Tux. Where's Tux?"

Oh God, please. Not the cat, too. Hasn't Mother suffered enough?

"I don't know, Mother. Maybe he got out. You know how skittish cats are." To the neighbors, she said, "Has anyone seen a black-and-white cat with a sparkly red collar?"

"And a jingle bell. He has a jingle bell," Frannie said desperately. "He's fond of birds."

A chorus of heads waggled a negative reply, faces full of sympathy.

"Never know, Mrs. Adler, he might show up after things die down. Cats don't like noise and commotion."

Frannie nodded without enthusiasm. She had faced an Alzheimer's diagnosis with humor, buried a husband with strength and resilience but today she looked defeated.

"What I am going to do, Carrie?" she muttered. "What in the world will I do?"

Most of Mother's memories, both tangible and emotional, had been inside that house. Now there was nothing solid left to hold her back from the empty chasm of Alzheimer's disease. No reminders, no photos, not even her beloved cat.

A tight fist of grief knotted in the center of her chest, Carrie said the only thing she could.

"You'll come home with me."

"This is only temporary, Carrie Ann, until I get back on my feet."

The declaration was more in character than anything Frannie had said or done all evening, though the air of defeat hanging on her was as heavy as the scent of smoke. The latter filled Carrie's house, overpowering the soft fragrance of vanilla potpourri.

"Fine, Mother. We'll start looking around for a new place as soon as you're ready." No need to say the obvious. With Alzheimer's closing in like a hungry wolf, her days of living independently had been numbered anyway. She was here, and here she would stay. "For now, this is your space. Do anything you want to with it."

She expected Frannie to make some remark about putting up silly posters or painting the ceiling with the solar system. Instead, her mother sat down on the end of the bed and removed her red hat, turning it over and over in her hands like a lost child.

"I'm grateful. Tell Dan I know this is a sacrifice."

"It's no sacrifice, Mother," Carrie lied, feeling guilty because Dan had not been against Mother moving in. The naysayer was her. Yet, what choice did they have under the circumstances? Mother could no longer take care of herself; that much was obvious from the fire. "We have tons of space."

They'd built this house in those early days when Lexi was tiny and hope remained for filling all the rooms. Over the years, they'd occasionally mention downsizing but the subject was a painful reminder of the children they'd never had, so they'd long ago stopped talking about it.

"I suppose I need a shower."

"We both do." But neither moved. Wanting to offer comfort, Carrie lingered, sick with sorrow and sympathy and a feeling of helplessness. "Would you like some iced tea? Or I could run down to the convenience store and get some Mountain Dew."

"No. I'm fine." Fran picked at the tulle on her hat. "Do you think Tux will turn up?"

Mother had thought of little else since the devastation. Not of her house or her clothes or thirty years of memories, but of the black-and-white tomcat. His disappearance seemed a poignant symbol that Fran would eventually lose everything near and dear.

"Dan and Lexi said they'd go back to the neighborhood after dinner and look for him. All the cars and fire trucks should be gone by then."

"He likes Lexi. He'll come out for her."

Pained by Mother's eternal optimism, Carrie figured there was nothing left of the gentle old cat to find.

Frannie leaned back on the pillows and let her red glittery slides fall to the floor. They'd found the lost shoe next to Frannie's car, safe and sound, the only pair to survive this day's events. Red hat, red shoes and a purple pantsuit. They would have to do.

"I'm tired." Mother closed her eyes.

Carrie had never seen her this down. The reaction was probably normal for most people, but not for Francis Adler.

She lingered in the doorway for another minute, watching her mother and wondering how to help her face the days ahead. Then, heart heavy, she headed for the kitchen to fix something quick to eat.

Everything was where she'd left it a few hours ago when she'd been happy and singing and preparing homemade ice cream. Now the half bowl of peeled peaches had turned an ugly brown and fruit flies swarmed around the sticky mess.

Dan appeared beneath the archway between the living and dining rooms. "Is she all right?"

Carrie propped a palm on the edge of the counter and leaned, glad for something sturdy to hold her up. "I don't know. She's resting."

"Good."

He looked the way she felt. Lost. Uncertain. She longed for him to take her in his arms and assure her that everything would be okay. She needed to cry, long and hard, while Dan rubbed her back and uttered those unintelligible man sounds that made her feel safe and loved.

"We should call Robby."

"He won't come. He'll leave everything up to us."

"Still, we should call."

Carrie knew Dan was right, but as experience had taught her, so was she.

"Life is so unfair," she murmured.

"Everything will work out."

Platitudes she did not want. Life only worked out when she fought and clawed and forced it to her will, something she couldn't do with Alzheimer's disease and house fires.

Frustrated, aching, despondent, she

turned to dump the ruined fruit into the garbage disposal.

"Carrie?"

"What?" Tears burned behind her nose. She sniffed.

"Are you going to be okay?"

Leaning hard against the sink, Carrie nodded. From the corner of her eye she could see him standing there, uncertain and bewildered, wishing he could fix this the way he fixed a car or a leaky faucet. "I'm fine."

He shifted, moved forward, then stopped. "I want to be what you need, honey, but I don't know what that is."

The torrent broke and in the next instant, Dan's strong, workman's arms went around her, pulling her close to his thudding heart. He said nothing, just held her while she wept.

And though it solved nothing, for now it was enough.

CHAPTER NINE

Fran moved through the house in a daze. It was such a big house, not like her bungalow. She stopped in the kitchen and gazed around. What was this? She should know but the word wouldn't come. And why had she come in here?

She stood in the center of the room and closed her eyes. "Father, I'm scared. I don't know what I'm doing. Don't tell Carrie. She freaks out."

She waited, listening to the quiet sounds of an empty house. Dan and Carrie were at work. Lexi had gone swimming with friends.

A moment ago her heart had been racing but now she began to calm. The Lord was here. His sweet, sweet spirit eased over her like a warm massage.

She opened her eyes, relieved to have the fog lifting. That was the awful thing about this forgetting disease. She knew the episode was happening, but she was helpless to stop it.

"Coffee!" She threw her hands into the air. "Thank you, Jesus." She'd come in here to make coffee.

After she'd filled the pot and set it to brew, the doorbell chimed. Drying her hands with one of Carrie's fancy dish towels, she went to answer it.

A familiar form stood beneath the covered entry, green John Deere cap and something else in hand. Her heart thudded once with a hope too foolish to acknowledge.

"Ken." How she'd missed that handsome face.

Without preamble, he said, "I made a mistake, Frannie."

The ember of hope flared up again. "You did?"

"Biggest mistake I've made in a long time, and I've made some doozies. Can I come in and talk to you? I'll understand if you give me the boot. I deserve it."

"Oh, silly, get in here." She plucked his sleeve and pulled, more glad to see him than he could ever know. "I guess you heard about my house."

"I did. Sure sorry about that."

"Burned it down myself. The Alzheimer's, they tell me. I left a pan on the stove."

"You're safe. That's all that matters."

"Sit, Ken." She motioned him toward the long, rolled-arm sofa. "Would you like some of Carrie's tea?"

"No, no. Nothing for me, thanks."

He moved past her, and as he did, Frannie caught a whiff of shower soap and English Leather. Her farmer had cleaned up to come calling.

"You sure you're all right?" he asked. He looked so concerned that she was nearly overcome with emotion.

"I'm very thankful. The Lord protected me from my silly self." She tried to make light of the tragedy, but even she could hear the ache in her voice.

Ken's indrawn breath was ragged. "When I heard your house burned . . ." He shook his head, jaw tight. "The news shook me up, got me thinking. What if you'd been inside?" He glanced up and then down again, voice low and regretful. "What if I'd lost you forever?"

Fran didn't say the obvious — that he would lose her anyway.

His grip tightened on the cap he held. His Adam's apple bobbed.

"All the color went out of my life without you, Frannie. The whole world turned gray, like it was after Ellen died." His eyes sought hers again and held on as though afraid to glance away lest she disappear. The notion filled her with poignant joy. "I missed you. Missed you more than I can ever explain. I'm sorry for being a scared old fool. Will you forgive me?"

Frannie settled next to him on Carrie's beige sofa, needing to touch him. "No forgiveness needed. I understood."

He made a sad, self-disparaging face. "I'd feel a lot better if you'd rake me over the coals a little, make me pay."

"Life's too short for that, Ken Markovich." She squeezed his biceps, the muscle firm and strong beneath her touch. "I'm just happy to see you again."

What an understatement. Though aware she was selfish to let him back into her life when the future was so terribly bleak, Fran couldn't bear to send him away.

"What are your plans?" he asked. "I mean, now that your house is gone? You're going to need a place to live."

"I have a place here with Dan and Carrie until I get on my feet again." She knew that would never happen, but admitting as much would be like surrendering to the disease. Francis Adler might be taken captive, but she would never surrender.

"I have a house. A big place that you've

always liked." Ken turned the green cap over, bending the bill into a vee. "Why not move in with me?"

Fran gave him a playful swat on the arm. Intentionally misunderstanding because she knew where he was leading, she fanned her face and laughed. "Why, Ken Markovich, I am not that kind of woman."

Ken wouldn't be put off by her foolishness. He tossed the cap aside and took her hand, his calloused fingers gentle. "Marry me, Frannie. Let me look after you."

Fran ached with regret as she slipped her hand from his and reached up to cradle his beloved face. "My dear, dear Ken. Because I love you, I will never marry you."

Pain shifted through the most sincere brown eyes she'd ever seen. "Alzheimer's disease makes no difference to me. You're still the light of my life."

She hated hurting him this way, but better now than for months and years to come. "You've already lost one wife to an ugly, unforgiving disease. I won't do that to you again."

"I want to."

Shaking her head, Fran dropped her hands to the smooth fabric of the couch, gripping the cushion for support. She glanced away from those searching eyes, struggling to do the right thing when she longed to fall into Ken's arms and say yes.

With sadness throbbing in her words, she murmured, "They tell me a time will come when I won't even know you. Oh, my darling, Ken. I won't even know you."

With farm-worn fingers, both rough and tender, Ken touched her cheek and brought her gaze back to his. Gently, he said, "But I'll know *you*, Frannie. I'll know you."

"I don't want to forget." The admission slipped out before she could think better of it. "I have so many wonderful memories. I don't want to forget."

Ken swallowed. His nostrils flared. "I've never been good at coming up with the right words, Fran. But there's things I want to say to you, things you need to hear. I found someone who said it all, exactly how I feel." He picked up a CD he'd placed on the coffee table and carried the disc to Carrie's stereo. "If I can figure out how this thing works."

He fiddled for a minute while Fran's heart beat against her ribs like a canary about to break loose from a cage. "What is it?"

"Be patient." His smile was self-conscious. "I'll get there."

She watched his thick fingers work, heard the click and whirr of the CD player. Ken turned, held her eyes with his.

"This is for you, Frannie." He touched his heart. "From me."

The gentle swell of orchestra music began and the honeyed tones of Nat King Cole singing "Unforgettable" filled the room with song.

Ken moved toward her, his lips mouthing the words.

After just a few bars, tears flowed down Fran's face and Ken was quick to cross the room, kneeling at her side. She cupped his dear, dear cheek with one hand and smiled as the song ended. Ken's weatherworn fingertips wiped away her tears and then gathered her into his embrace.

With a bittersweet ache for what could never be, Fran rested against him, saying nothing, for indeed, there was nothing left to say.

Chapter Ten

If Carrie thought the situation with Mother would improve in the days following the fire, she was wrong. So wrong that she began to dread waking up in the mornings. Her part-time work at the library was her only reprieve, although she worried about Frannie every moment. Mother had always been unpredictable and spontaneous. That hadn't changed. The difference was in her ability to comprehend her own behavior. She had hours of perfect lucidity and then in an instant, she would change into a stranger with a blank stare. It was terrifying and heartrending.

One night, long after Mother had beat them all at a game of Scrabble and called it a night Carrie took solace in the soothing task of folding freshly washed laundry. Cleaning always calmed her, made her feel in control again whether she was or not. And Heaven knew, she was not in control.

Carrying a load of Downy-scented towels to Mother's bathroom, she heard voices coming through the bedroom door. She paused to listen. Was Mother on the phone? Or praying perhaps? It wouldn't be the first time Carrie had heard her mother talking aloud to God as if He were in the room. Not wanting to disturb her, Carrie quietly leaned her ear against the door.

"Your mother is under a lot of stress, rosebud," she heard Frannie say. "We have to keep praying for her."

Carrie pressed the towels closer, her pulse jump-started to be the topic of conversation between her daughter and her mother.

"But you're the one losing your memory," Lexi's light, youthful voice said.

"She's the one having to deal with forgetful old me. It's hard to be in her shoes. And I think she's still angry with the church."

Mother had that right.

"Do you think Mom is mad at God, too?"

Carrie stiffened, awaiting her mother's reply. If this wasn't her daughter talking, she'd barge in there and let them have it for gossiping behind her back.

"I hope not, darling. Without the Lord, none of us will get through this in one piece. The last thing I ever wanted was to be a burden on my kids."

"You could never be a burden, Grannie Frannie." The bed groaned as if someone had sat down. "You're as much fun as ever. Even Mr. Markovich must think so. He sure comes over a lot."

Mother's warm chuckle filtered beneath the door. "He's a good man. When I get too crazy to remember my name, you treat him nicely, okay? He's going to be pretty sad."

"I'll be sad, too, Gran. Real sad."

"But oh, my precious, we have some fine memories, don't we? Lots and lots of fine memories. And we're going to make lots more before I check out of here for good. You think on those instead of being sad." A soft, patting sound. "Okay?"

"Okay." Lexi's voice was muffled as though she'd leaned into her grandmother's fleshy arms. "I was thinking about doing a research paper on AD. Is that all right with you?"

"A splendid idea, rosebud. I'll be your guinea pig. I've been doing some research myself. It's not pretty."

"I know. I don't want you to lose your memory, Gran."

"Me, either, but you and I both know that God will take care of us. Right?"

"Right."

"You're a smart little chickie, you know that?"

"I take after my gran."

The statement sent a spear through Carrie. What if her precious only child carried the Alzheimer's gene? How unfair would that be?

The anger beneath the surface bubbled up again. She turned from the closed door and walked away.

A week after the fire, Carrie, Lexi, and Frannie spent the day shopping. Afterward, Frannie had sprung for banana splits at the ice-cream shop where Lexi's new boyfriend worked. The trio sat talking about Frannie's new but equally gaudy wardrobe, Lexi's sports banquet they'd attended on Saturday night, and the upcoming music festival at church.

When Carrie's cell phone rang inside her purse, Lexi dived for it. "It's for me."

"Probably." Carrie smiled around a mouthful of butter-pecan ice cream. She was beginning to see the wisdom of getting Lexi her own phone. Nine calls out of ten were for her anyway.

Turning slightly to one side, an action Carrie found amusing considering she and Frannie could hear every word, Lexi spoke into the tiny mouthpiece. A second later, she turned back and caught her mother's gaze. Carrie put down her spoon.

"What?" she mouthed.

Lexi shook her head and held up one finger. "That's awesome. Thanks for calling." She snapped the device closed. "Good news. Someone spotted a black-and-white cat sniffing around the ashes of Grannie's house."

Frannie clasped both hands to her chest. "Oh, praise the Lord. Let's go."

She was already moving out of the booth. Carrie grabbed her purse and followed, hoping her mother wasn't going to be disappointed again.

The short drive to the old neighborhood was filled with anticipatory tension and speculation between Lexi and Fran about where Tux had been hiding out all this time. Carrie kept her mouth shut, the pessimist in her already trying to think of ways to soothe the hurt when Tux was nowhere to be seen.

As they pulled into the driveway, Fran's chipper countenance quieted. Seeing the burned-out home always affected her.

They parked at the edge of the drive and got out.

"Here kitty, kitty." Lexi immediately

301

started to walk around the perimeter.

"Stay away from all that junk, Lexi," Carrie admonished, reminding herself to call the insurance company and find out when they were going to have the lot cleaned off. "There could be snakes in there."

Snakes maybe, but no sign of the cat.

"Tux, come on Tuxedo. Tux!" Frannie moved in the opposite direction, calling and making smoochie sounds with her mouth.

The ever-present knot in Carrie's shoulder tightened. Where was that stupid cat? Dan had spent hours combing through the ashes and wreckage but found no remains. He considered that a good sign. Carrie figured the cat was cremated along with so many of her mother's other belongings.

"Mom! Grannie!" Lexi's excited voice came from behind a dilapidated shed. Carrie's nerves jumped. Her first thought was, a snake. "He's out here. I found him."

Frannie's head jerked toward Carrie. With a whoop and an arm upraised in victory, she galloped toward the shed.

CHAPTER ELEVEN

By the time they arrived home, the dirty cat purring happily in Frannie's lap, Carrie felt more positive than she had in months. Tux had lost weight but he was alive, and Mother had had a very good day. Even Frannie remarked that she hadn't been "crazy" today. She and Lexi had giggled at the remark. Carrie didn't see the humor.

Though a cat in the house was not her idea of a good thing, Carrie didn't protest when Frannie carried Tux straight to the kitchen for a bowl of milk and a can of Vienna sausages.

"I'll have to get out to Wal-Mart for cat food and flea spray," her mother said. "Poor baby, he's probably covered."

Oh joy.

Tux ate greedily and after accepting a few more ear rubs and hugs, slithered away to curl up and sleep in Dan's chair. Carrie refused to think about the fleas jumping off into the upholstery.

Humming happily, Mother took her shopping bags down the hall to her bedroom. She returned wearing one of the new outfits, an almost sedate turquoise pantsuit with sequin-lined collar and cuffs. "How do I look?"

"Wonderful." Carrie leaned forward and hugged her mother's shoulders.

"Good, because I feel like celebrating. Tux has come safely home. God is good. I have a glorious new outfit. Hand me that telephone. I'm going to call Roland and invite him to a movie."

Carrie froze. Roland again.

"Mother," she started.

"Who's Roland, Grannie?" Seated on the sofa across from the sleeping cat, Lexi had one foot propped on her knee as she applied polish to her toenails. She looked up with a grin. "Does Mr. Markovich know you've got another boyfriend on the string?"

Carrie shook her head at Lexi.

Her daughter frowned, head tilted in bewilderment. "What?"

"Roland was mother's boyfriend a long time ago. Remember, Mother?" she said to Fran. "Roland was a long time ago."

Frannie's animated expression turned to confusion. "He was?"

"Yes. You and Roland broke up. You married Daddy. He died. Remember?"

Lexi capped the fingernail polish and set the bottle on the coffee table. The snick of glass against wood sounded loud. She stared from her mother to her grandmother and back again as comprehension dawned. Her pretty face filled with the sad knowledge, slicing off a chunk of Carrie's pounding heart.

"Grannie," she said softly, rising from the couch to stand beside her grandmother. "Are you okay?"

"I slipped again, didn't I?"

A thick silence clouded the room.

Frannie went to the sofa, sitting with a heavy sigh. "I feel so stupid. I don't know what made me think of Roland. That's the thing about this forgetting disease. It makes me feel stupid."

"You're probably tired, Mother. I know I am. Today has been a busy day. A good day, too. We found Tux." Her throat ached with unspent emotion.

Frannie didn't answer, but Carrie could see she was bothered and didn't want to be. Watching her chipper nature struggle to rise above her problems was heartbreaking.

"Grannie Frannie, do you remember how to make cobbler?" Lexi asked.

"Well, of course I do. Making cobbler is a piece of cake." She and Lexi stared at each other for one beat and then burst out laughing. Carrie chuckled with them, and the painful moment passed.

"Do we still have berries in the freezer?" Lexi said to Carrie.

"Tons of them, thanks to Mr. Blanton's abundant garden."

"Awesome. I'll get the video camera." She hopped up and left the room, returning with the device. "Come on, Grannie. You're going to teach me how to make cobbler while you still remember."

"Lexi!" Carrie felt uncomfortable being so bold about her mother's disease. Her daughter was far less inhibited.

Neither Lexi or Frannie paid her one bit of attention.

"And you'll videotape my recipe?" Mother asked.

At Lexi's nod, a wide grin creased Frannie's face. "Splendid idea, rosebud. You are such a blessing. Let me change out of my glamour girl attire and get my hat. Oh wait. I don't have a chef hat anymore." She tapped a finger against her cheek and then inspiration struck. "I know just the thing."

Carrie rolled her eyes heavenward. Mother had haunted the secondhand stores for hats, coming home with some wild and wacky headgear. "Cooking? In one of your hats?"

"I think it's a great idea, Mom." Lexi's eyes pleaded with her to go along with the game. Carrie's heart constricted. Her teen-age daughter, like her mother, was trying to make the most of a bad situation.

All right. She could do this. She *would* do this, for Lexi and Mother. Forcing a cheerfulness she didn't feel, Carrie went to the freezer for berries.

Even with Mother's momentary regression, the unexpected return of Tux put a renewed zip in everyone's spirits. Early the next Saturday morning, Frannie sailed away in The Tanker with a promise to return in time for lunch, and though Carrie suffered a pinch of concern, she simply waved goodbye and got busy cleaning out the kitchen cabinets.

Dan and his growing troop of boys, along with Lexi and Courtney, were out in the backyard hammering away on a doghouse for B.J.'s beagle. Carrie gazed out the dining room window watching the beehive of activity, all the while thinking this was the way life should have been — Dan with a bevy of kids to love and teach. Had things turned out differently, the way she'd wanted them to, those boys could have been Dan's to share his skills and knowledge and absorb his stalwart, manly kind of love.

He said something to Lexi and she nodded, then separated from the mass and came toward the house.

"I guess you're all getting hungry," Carrie said as soon as Lexi opened the back door.

"Dad wants to know if you'll make sandwiches for everyone."

"Sure."

"I'll help. The guys think they're dying of starvation."

Carrie shook her head with a smile as she pulled sandwich fixings from the fridge. "How's the doghouse coming?"

"We're about done. Dad says we might start building them all the time to sell and then use the money to take the boys camping or something."

"Good idea and really nice of your dad to think of it."

"Yeah. Grannie Frannie says mentoring boys is Dad's ministry."

Carrie cocked her head. Dan didn't even go to church. How could he have a ministry? "Really? Did you tell your dad that?"

"Yeah. He said maybe she was right. And you know what else he said?"

"I can't imagine."

"He said maybe that's why I never had brothers, because God knew there would be boys who needed him and if he already had a bunch of other kids he might be too busy."

Slathering mayo on a slice of bread, Carrie paused to stare into the gray-blue depths of her daughter's eyes and then to gaze out into her backyard at the circle of man and boys. Dan laughed and draped an arm over B.J.'s shoulders, hugging the thin child to his side. Her husband had a ministry to boys. He wasn't mourning the lack of babies. He was happy and fulfilled and doing exactly what he needed and wanted to do, and she hadn't even realized it.

Carrie finished the sandwiches and called everyone in for lunch. She was so bemused by the revelation that she didn't think about her mother's absence until Dan mentioned it.

"She said she'd be back for lunch." Carrie glanced at the clock on the microwave. The digits read twelve-thirty. "She'll be here soon."

But she wasn't. And by the time one-thirty rolled around, Carrie's prickle of anxiety had grown to near panic. She phoned Alice and then Ken, neither of whom had seen Frannie.

"I shouldn't have let her go alone," she

said to Dan. "I should have gone with her."

Dan's frown indicated his concern. "She goes by herself all the time. She's probably shopping and lost track of time."

Carrie didn't say the obvious. Mother could lose track of everything. "I'm worried, Dan. Anything could happen."

"The kids and I will scatter out around the neighborhood and then go downtown, see if we can spot her car."

"Good idea. I'll stay here in case she calls or comes in. Take the cell phone with you. Lexi, you and Courtney walk over to the old neighborhood. She might have gone back there by instinct."

Dan put on his baseball cap and went to the door. Four boys imitated his every move, adjusting caps on their own heads. "If she doesn't show up by two, I think you should call the police."

Carrie nodded grimly.

"And it wouldn't hurt to pray, either," he said, shocking her, right before he closed the door.

Pray. What good would prayer do? But in desperation, she tossed up a halfhearted request for her mother's safety, then got out the phone book and started calling all of Frannie's friends.

At two o'clock she called the police,

humiliated by proxy for her mother. Then she cleaned the oven.

At four o'clock Dan and the kids returned, tired and thirsty and worried. After fixing lemonade for the troops, Carrie mopped the kitchen.

By a quarter to five, she was convinced something terrible had happened. "What if Mother is like one of those people you hear about who wander off and are found years later and hundreds of miles away? Or worse yet —"

The sound of a car door stopped her. Lexi rushed to the window. "It's Mr. Markovich." She yanked the door open. "And Grannie!"

Relief shuddered through the room as everyone rushed to the door. Ken Markovich, looking sad, gently held Mother's hand as he led her across the yard to the porch.

Frannie seemed dazed, her hair mussed, her makeup smeared.

"Mother, what happened? Where have you been?"

Ken answered for her. "Frannie got a little lost. She's tired." He led her mother into the house and to the sofa, his voice gentle and coaxing. "Sit down and rest, Frannie. You've had a long day. Carrie will bring you a Mountain Dew. You're home. Everything is okay now."

Carrie had a dozen questions, but Ken was right. Mother was safe and the story of what had happened could come later. "Dan, will you phone the police and let them know she's all right?"

Dan nodded and went to the phone. Carrie brought glasses of soda for Ken and her mother, sick with a despair reflected on Ken's kindly face.

And so another of the last straws had broken as Mother's independence was being stripped away, one thing at a time.

Later, after Ken had left, Fran surrendered her car keys, declaring The Tanker now belonged to Lexi. Though she tried to put on a happy face, she, too, was clearly devastated by the latest turn of events. Ken had found her walking down a country road, six miles from where she'd left her car parked at the mall. At first, she hadn't known who he was.

Just when Carrie had thought things were getting better, the bottom had fallen out again. And she realized this was the way the rest of Mother's life would be — one heartache after another.

That night after the lights were out, she lay in bed staring into the darkness, too miserable to sleep. Dan was still awake, too. She could hear him breathing, feel his alertness.

"Want to talk about it?" he said, without touching her.

Her hair made swishing sounds against the pillow as she shook her head. "What's the use? I'm losing my mother in increments and things are only going to get worse. Talking won't fix it."

"For her sake, we should try to stay positive."

"I can't. I'm too angry."

"At your mom? Or me?"

"Oh, Dan. Neither." She shifted in frustration. "I don't know. The church. God. Someone. It just burns me up that Mother has spent her life doing good. I've decided God doesn't pay one bit of attention to anything we do down here. He has no idea how many years of service she's given to that church or how many pennies she's pinched to send someone else's kids to Bible camp."

"Blaming God isn't going to solve anything."

"I can't help it."

"For your mom you need to try. Do you know what she wants most of all?" He shifted toward her in the darkness. She felt his warm breath on her cheek. "She wants you and me and Lexi to find the joy in living that she has. She wants us to see God's wonders and grace all around us."

"And where would that be? There's nothing wonderful about Alzheimer's disease or spending the day searching for your lost mother. Everything is bleak and ugly and horrible right now."

"But there are positives, too. Your mom would want us to think about those."

"I can't think of a single one."

"All right, then, let me help you. Ken found your mom before anything terrible happened. She was spared from that fire. She could have died just as easily. We found the cat, a miracle right there, all things considered."

Carrie was silent for a few minutes, listening to the hum of air-conditioning through the vents. She knew Dan was right in some ways but if God really cared, why was this happening at all?

"I've been thinking about something else, too," Dan said, the rumble of his voice quiet and comforting in the darkness.

"What?" she mumbled.

"Church."

Carrie's jaw tightened. "Bunch of hypocrites, just like you always said."

"I was wrong."

"No, you were right. I'm not going to

church anymore."

Dan huffed in disgust. "Who are you punishing, Carrie? God? Yourself? Because this anger is getting you nowhere."

Carrie turned over and buried her face in the pillow. She didn't know the answer and probably never would. But she couldn't go on attending church and pretending that everything was fine.

CHAPTER TWELVE

All day Sunday a pall hung over the house. No one went to church, not even Frannie and Lexi, though the latter wondered aloud about the change in routine. Carrie muttered something about letting Grannie rest, and then she cooked roast beef with mashed potatoes and brown gravy and fresh yeast rolls, but no one ate much. After lunch, Dan took his rod and reel and went fishing. Everyone else moped around, quiet and depressed, so that when the doorbell chimed, Carrie was tempted not to answer. Lexi answered for her.

"Mom, we have company."

"Great." She hoped she sounded more enthused than she felt. Drying her hands on a dish towel, she took the extra seconds to fold the thick terry cloth carefully over the oven handle before going to the living room. As she entered she heard her mother's cheery voice.

"Come in, come in. Oh, my goodness' sakes alive, what a treat to see you."

A dozen or more women from the church trailed into the house, each carrying something.

"I hope you don't mind the surprise call," Candace Ellis, the pastor's wife, said. "We've been working on this for a while, but the time never felt right. So when you weren't at church this morning, well, this just seemed to be the day."

"For what?" Carrie asked, bewildered by the smiling ladies she'd intentionally avoided this morning.

"We are the unofficial Memory Lane Committee. After Fran's house burned and well, her illness and all, we got to thinking of some way we could help out."

Alice, Mother's closest friend, cleared her throat and lofted a bulging photo album, eyes shining with love and a hint of tears. "Memories. Losing your memories, whether in your brain or in your house is just a rotten shame. So we, the Memory Lane Committee, are resurrecting old memories of the fabulous, unforgettable Frannie Adler." She shot a grin toward Frannie. "The two of us have been all over this state having fun, and I have the proof right here." She slapped the cover of the album. "The other ladies have photos and ticket stubs and all kinds of memorabilia of Fran's life, too. Carrie, some of these things even include you and Robby as kids."

Carrie's hand went to her suddenly full throat. "Oh my. Oh my gracious."

Fran laughed. "I think you've overwhelmed her, girls. Come on, let's move this shindig to the kitchen table. I can't wait to get my paws on what you've dug up. I may not remember them in my head, but I'll remember when I see them."

None of the ladies seemed the least put off by Frannie's blunt appraisal of her declining faculties.

Once in the dining room, the women, still dressed in their Sunday best, began to unveil their findings.

"Some folks didn't have pictures so they wrote stories about some of the funny, entertaining, or wonderfully kind things they remember about Frannie. They're in here." Rhonda Flanders presented a notebook, beautifully hand-covered in lace and fabric, to Frannie. For once, Carrie thought the woman's long hair and narrow face looked lovely. "We thought we all might enjoy doing a scrapbooking project together with the rest of the stuff."

"Is that okay with you?" Candace asked,

glancing at Carrie. "Dan thought it was a good idea when I called a bit ago."

No wonder Dan had gone fishing. The sweet, sneaky man. "This is wonderful and the timing couldn't be better. Mother had a rough day yesterday."

"I got lost," Frannie said without batting an eye.

Alice laughed as if Fran had said something funny. Sometimes, most times, Carrie did not understand Mother and her friends.

"Well, you're found today," Alice said. "So let's get at it. Going through this stuff is going to be a hoot and a half, just like you."

"Bring it on, sister." Frannie pumped the air with her fist and then scraped back a chair and plopped down, eager as a child, while Alice dumped a box of odds and ends on the table.

Lexi sidled up beside her grandmother and slid an arm over her shoulders. "Wow, Grannie Frannie, this is awesome. Look at all this stuff."

She picked up an ancient photo of a slimmer, younger Frannie driving a go-cart at an amusement park, a very small child seated next to her. "That's me. I remember that. Grannie bought me cotton candy. I laid it in the seat and a fat lady sat on it. Grannie laughed and laughed and laughed when the lady walked away with pink fluff stuck to the behind of her black shorts."

Fran chortled. "Yes, and this little minx laughed, too. Don't let her fool you with that innocent smile." Frannie patted Lexi's hand. "Made me buy her more cotton candy, too."

Amused chuckles circled the room.

"You have to write that down, honey," Carrie said to Lexi, her voice soft with nostalgia. "It's exactly the kind of memory your grandmother wants to keep. And look at this." She tapped a photo of herself in a hideous pair of expensive boots that had been all the fad when she was thirteen. Her mother had worked an extra job to pay for the long-forgotten clodhoppers. "I can't believe I wanted those so badly."

"Eek, Mom, you look like a geek."

Carrie snickered, though her throat was still tight with emotion. "I'm afraid you're right. But I thought I was so cool then."

"Does that mean, I'll look back someday and think I look geeky?"

"Yep." She hooked an elbow around her daughter's neck. "Sure does."

Frannie herself stared moist-eyed at the array of memories from her life — photos, ticket stubs, oversize printed buttons from various festivals, bumper stickers, recipes.

"I thought everything was lost in the fire," she said in wonder, brightly polished nails trailing over one thing after another. "I was afraid they were gone forever and I wouldn't be able to remember any of them."

"Well, girlfriend," Alice said, bumping Fran with her hip. "When you forget, we'll remember. Between the lot of us, we should be able to stay afloat. Look at this one of you and Jake. You're skinny as a stick."

Fran's bawdy laugh returned. "I've never been skinny a day in my life."

Carrie leaned in. She'd seen so few photos of the father who had died before she had memories. "He looks like Robby."

"Was he a hippie or something, Grannie?" Lexi asked.

"Mercy, no. Everyone wore long hair and striped bell-bottoms back then. Handsome rascal, wasn't he?"

While they dug through and sorted out the box of memorabilia, two of the ladies carried in snacks and drinks and before Carrie realized what was happening, a full-scale party was in swing. There was laughter and tears, jokes and silliness. Most of all, she felt the love being poured out upon her mother by the women Carrie had considered hypocritical and uncaring.

"Carrie, honey," Kathleen Filbert said, her

dyed red hair startling beneath the glare of the dining room chandelier. "Look at this photo. You were the most adorable little girl. One time when you were maybe six or seven your mama took you to an Easter egg hunt, all dressed up in one of those fluffy dresses, and the newspaper took your picture. Put it right on the front page. Do you remember that, Frannie?"

"I think I saw that clipping in here somewhere," Candace said and started digging. She found the yellow newsprint with a whoop, waving it under Frannie's nose.

Carrie remembered. Mother had made that fluffy pink dress herself, spending hours after work hand sewing lace and frills so her little girl could look as pretty as the rich kids.

In fact, a flood of beautiful memories, long forgotten, came sweeping in. She and her mother and Robby joyfully dancing around a tiny Christmas tree, wearing paper Santa hats and licking candy canes, so happy they couldn't stop grinning, and having no idea that their mother had pawned her wedding rings to buy the gifts. Later that day, people from the church had dropped by, loaded with turkey and all the trimmings. And that wasn't the only time the church had come to the rescue. Then she'd been humiliated, but now she understood. They were doing the ministry of Christ in the only way they knew how.

Tears gathered in the corners of her eyes. The deep throb of bitterness began to ease. She'd been wrong. These ordinary, fallible women, with their funny stories and cupcakes were showing love, the Christ kind of love, God in action.

Realization swept through her. She was the problem, not God, not the church. Her. Carrie Martin.

With a mumbled, "excuse me," she left the noisy, cheery dining room and went into the bathroom where she let the tears come. Cleansing tears of release and repentance.

"Lord God in Heaven, I've been so angry at You when all along my attitude was the problem. Forgive me. Help me to find the extravagant faith and joy my mother has."

She prayed for a long time, for her mother, her family, her relationship with Dan. Most of all, she prayed to know God for who He really was, not who she imagined Him to be. When the storm of tears and prayer subsided, she sat on the cold, hard edge of the bathtub, feeling drained but strangely and wonderfully refreshed.

A knock sounded on the door. "Mom, are you okay?"

"Better than I've been in a long time," she replied and stepped out into the hall with a shiny nose, reddened eyes and a smile.

Life wasn't perfect and never would be, no matter how hard she worked, but today had taught her something valuable. Life happened one moment at a time, one memory at a time. Every minute she spent in anger and bitterness was a minute she should be making memories, loving, giving, because once that moment was gone, memories were all she'd have left.

CHAPTER THIRTEEN

Fran awoke in the strange, unfamiliar bedroom, more afraid than she'd ever been in her life. Blood pounded against her temples. Where was she? Had she been kidnapped? Whose were those voices she could hear? Afraid to move or make noise, she stared around the room, trying to remember. The fog was thick this morning, as if she'd awakened in . . . Where was that city with the heavy fog? Frustrated, she let it go. It didn't matter. She was lost and alone.

Her frantic gaze fell on a book lying on the bedside table. Finally, something that looked familiar. As quietly as possible, she reached out and took the book in hand.

"My book. My Bible." The fog began to clear, enough that Fran realized she was having an episode. She couldn't bring the rest to mind but a name appeared and she clung to that single word like the life preserver it was. "Jesus."

She clutched the worn black book to her chest. "You promised to help me bear anything that came my way. If You could bear the cross, I can bear this." Tears welled. "What if I forget You, Father? That's the thing I fear the most. Don't let me forget You."

The bedside clock read nine, though Fran wasn't certain if that meant morning or night. She sat up and with trembling fingers opened the book to a random page in Isaiah and began to read.

Surely they may forget, yet I will not forget you. See, I have inscribed you on the palms of My hands.

Fran blinked and read the verses again, and as she did, the words pierced the remaining fog. She read them again and yet again. Relief and wonder started as a small bubble and grew into a giant balloon of renewed joy.

She might forget Him but God never would her. For all eternity, her name was written in the palms of His hands.

Tears of joy and gratitude and worship filled her eyes as fear was chased away by the unfathomable love of God. Fear of the future was forever gone, replaced by trust and assurance and an inexplicable peace.

"Thank you, Lord. Thank you."

She listened quietly, feeling the love envelop her like a warmth, hearing the still, small voice that had been her strength and guide since she'd accepted Christ at twelve years old.

After a long, sweet time, she pushed the covers aside, shoved her feet into bunny slippers and went to tell Carrie the great good news. She found her daughter, as always, cleaning something in an ever-spotless house.

"You know what?" she said without fanfare.

Carrie kept right on dusting the piano. The smell of lemon Pledge tickled Fran's nose. "Would you like some breakfast, Mother?"

"No, honey. I've already eaten."

Carrie arched an eyebrow. Frannie grinned.

"Feasting on the Word of God." At Carrie's softened expression, she went on. "I was back there praying and God said, 'Frannie, haven't I always taken care of you?' And I said, 'Yes, Lord, you always have.' And He said, 'Then get up, wash your face and get on with life. You still have work to do.' And He told me something else, too. I want to share it with you."

Carrie paused in her dusting, one hand on the cloth, the other on the Pledge can, finger on the trigger. "God never talks to me that way."

"He would if you'd listen. Here. I want to show you something." She flopped the well-worn Bible open and poked a chubby finger at a verse. "Right there it is."

Carrie leaned forward and squinted at the small print. What she read made her insides leap. "Surely they may forget, yet I will not forget you. See, I have inscribed you on the palms of My hands."

Tears clogged the back of her throat. "Mother, that's beautiful. I've never read that before."

Frannie hugged her daughter's waist. "God loves us so much, He jotted a note about us on His hands." Her voice softened as she seemed to quote. "What manner of love is this, that we should be called the children of God."

"Is that in the Bible, too?"

"Yep. Somewhere. I forget." Mother laughed. "One thing about Alzheimer's is that everything is always new. No matter how many times I read the Bible, something new and fresh pops up just when I need it. That's the way God is, always there, ready and eager to meet our needs in whatever way is best for us."

"I never thought of God that way. He always seemed to be about following rules and doing the right things." She spritzed a dull place on the table and rubbed hard.

"I know, honey. But God isn't into how much you *do,* as much as He's interested in how much you *love.*"

Carrie gave her mother's words some thought. Frannie had lived her life this way, loving and serving and never expecting anything in return. Somewhere Carrie had missed out on having that kind of relationship with Jesus.

"I'm nearly forty-two years old and I never knew God wanted to have a relationship with me. I just thought He wanted me to obey and serve Him and hope like crazy that I was good enough to get to Heaven."

"Oh, honey, a relationship with God is so much more, so much better than that. Now that you know better, you can really get to know Him instead of trying to win His approval by doing stuff. He already approves of you. He thinks you're fabulous, all because you believe in His Son, Jesus. He wants to fellowship with you, to be the Father you never had. Somewhere I failed in teaching you that, but having Alzheimer's has given me a second chance."

Carrie waved the dust cloth like a warning flag. "Mother, please. Don't credit this awful disease with anything good."

"I most certainly will. In a way, Alzheimer's is a gift and I'm going to be thankful for it. Remember Amy Crayton? One day she was on her front porch arguing with Cindy Raymond about a recipe for meat loaf, and the next day she fell over dead in her pink azaleas from a massive coronary."

"I don't see the point."

"Amy never knew the end was coming and that she had spent the last day of her life in a snit with her best friend over something as silly as meat loaf. I have this great gift from God, this ability to see the end. I have time to tell everyone how much I love them, time to share the love of Jesus with you. Time to say my goodbyes and to do a lot of things I've always wanted to do."

"I wish you didn't have to do this at all."

"But I do. End of subject. So instead of spitting against the wind and being miserable, let's try to see the good that can come out of it."

"You sound like Dan."

"He's a fine man. A fine *Christian* man."

Carrie smiled. A month ago the assertion would have shocked her but she was seeing faith in a whole new way. Even if Dan didn't fit her narrow definition of what a Christian should be, he was a man of faith who loved and served God.

"Just think, Carrie Ann, our incredible, extravagantly loving God has granted me the ability to realize that today is all I have. Don't you see what a gift that is? If we all knew that this day, this hour, this second was our last, wouldn't we live it to the fullest?"

The phrasing hit a chord with Carrie. Since the Memory Lane party, she'd been doing a lot of thinking about that very thing. One moment at a time was all any of them had. All any of them had ever had. She just hadn't realized it before.

"You know, Mother," she said, dropping the dust cloth onto the table. "I hate this disease. I hate seeing this happen to you. But maybe you're right."

"Good. I need some coffee."

"The pot is still fresh." She followed Fran into the kitchen and leaned on the cabinet.

A cup clattered onto the counter as Fran poured and sugared. "Did I tell you that Ken ordered a Harley?"

"A motorcycle? Ken Markovich? What on earth possessed him to do such a thing?"

"He always wanted one. I told him there is no time like the present. So he ordered one. A big one with all the gadgets and room for two."

"You aren't going to ride it, are you?" She knew the answer before Fran opened her mouth.

"Of course, I am. I have no reason to fear anything anymore, Carrie."

"As if you ever did."

"Oh, I did. I just didn't let you know about it."

"Really?" Now this was a surprise.

But Frannie only replied with a Cheshire smile. "This fall, after harvest, Ken's taking me to New England to see the foliage and the whales. Won't that be marvelous? I've always wanted to see those magnificent giants of the sea."

"I've heard the leaves are glorious."

"You and Dan should go, too. Maybe take Lexi and a couple of those little boys along for the ride."

Dan's "boys," as she'd come to think of them, had woven a path into her heart and she'd come to enjoy having them around. She and Dan had even discussed signing up for foster care. She smiled at the thought. Yes, she'd like that very much — she and Dan with their own personal ministry to kids.

Carrie opened a cabinet and reached for a

coffee mug. "I'm not buying a motorcycle."

Fran snickered. "Then go in a plane or a car, but go, honey. Go. Live. Enjoy. It's all going to be over so fast. I don't want you to miss a moment of this amazing, incredible, beautiful thing called life."

Carrie poured the still-hot, fragrant brew, cooling it with cream while she considered this morning's interesting revelations. "Mother?"

"What, honey?"

"I want you to know that I've been wrong about a lot of things. This morning you've really opened my eyes. And I want you to forgive all the stupid, selfish things I've said and done."

Her mother paused midsip, looking at her over the rim of the cup. "All I ever wanted was to see my children happy and fulfilled and walking in the amazing grace of God."

"I know. During the past few months, I've learned a lot of lessons. I've watched you struggle with this frightening disease and face it head-on, full of courage and faith while I whined and grew bitter. I want you to know that your way is the best way, and from now on I'm going to try to be more like you — loving, faithful, and maybe even a little outrageous."

The corners of Fran's lips twitched. "Oh

you are, are you?"

"Yeah. I are." She grinned at the purposeful grammar gaffe.

Fran pulled Carrie's face down and planted a noisy kiss on her forehead, a twinkle in her eyes. The scent of coffee circled them like one of Frannie's fragrant scarves. "Then I have a great idea."

Carrie drew back, smiling. "Do I want to hear this?"

Her mother's rich laugh filled the room. "Brace yourself, darling, because I'm going skydiving. And I want you to go with me."

CHAPTER FOURTEEN

Fran looked down, pulse thrumming in her temples, excited beyond expectation, but she wasn't afraid. Oh, no, she would never be afraid again. The sound of the airplane engine roared loudly in her ears, drowning out the sound of her thudding heart.

Her friends were down there, gathered like ants around the edge of the jump zone. She smiled. Ken stood out, a beacon in his green John Deere cap.

The fog moved in behind her eyelids but she fought it. Not today. She wanted to remember this moment when she'd finally brought her daughter to a place of free-falling on Jesus, totally trusting in God, for that's the way she viewed this new willing-ness in Carrie to do something outrageous and a little dangerous.

Her eyes found the green cap again. Ro-land. No, no, not Roland. Ken, holding a sign as he held her heart. A sign that read,

Unforgettable.

She focused in on that one word. Unforgettable. God would never, ever forget. She was written on the palms of His hands.

Carrie stood in the open doorway of the airplane, heart thundering in her ears. A million butterflies flapped and danced in her stomach. Excited, more than a little tense, but exhilarated beyond her wildest imaginings and wonderfully free.

The jump instructor stood next to her, checking and rechecking, repeating instructions they'd been practicing for days. She knew what to do. And as scary and crazy as it seemed, she wanted to. She only hoped, for Mother's sake, she could go through with the jump.

Down below, a crowd of well-wishers waved, and though she couldn't hear them, she knew they cheered. Friends, church members, Dan's boys and the Red Hat Society in full regalia had come out to celebrate this glorious, golden day with Fran and Carrie. Lexi was down there somewhere with Dan and her video camera, capturing every moment so they could all remember forever the day Carrie Martin shed her constricting cocoon and became as free-wheeling as her mother.

She turned her head, heavy in the protective helmet and met her mother's excited eyes. It occurred to her that jumping from an airplane was a lot like the journey into Alzheimer's. Once begun, there was no turning back and no safety net. And no matter how much they learned and studied, there would always be that element of fear and danger and the unpredictable.

The pilot gave the signal. The instructor nodded. Carrie's heart slammed against her rib cage.

"Mother, are you sure you want to do this?" Carrie shouted above the buffeting wind, hearing the anxiety in her voice. For a moment, she hoped her mother would back out. It was a long, long way to the ground.

Bulky in her jump attire and colorful parachute, Carrie's mother turned and cradled her daughter's face in her wrinkled hands. A soft smile lit Frannie's eyes as if she was looking at a child.

Maybe she was.

"Oh, baby," she said. "Don't be afraid. Just jump. Mama will hold your hand all the way down."

Carrie drew in her mother's love and courage like a breath of fresh air. She could do this. She wanted to. "I love you, Mom."

Frannie winked. "I love you, too."

And so, hand in hand, they took the leap, flying into the vast unknown together, secure in the knowledge that come what may, God would be with them, holding their hands, all the way down.

Dear Reader,

Mother's Day has become a day of reflection for me. I tend to drag out the photo albums and leaf through, dripping a tear or two on the faded pages of my life. In memory, I relive those precious moments of the first tooth, the first step, and even of that first time one of my baby birds flew the nest, leaving behind a hole that would never be filled again. Yet, as painful as the loss, there's a fulfillment there, too, in knowing that I gave my children wings, taught them to fly, and they soared into adulthood, confident and healthy.

Jacqueline Kennedy was once quoted as saying, "If you bungle raising your children, I don't think whatever else you do well matters very much." That sums up my feelings toward motherhood, too. So when Mother's Day arrives, along with my kids and their families, I say a heartfelt thanks to God because somehow, someway, I didn't bungle the most significant job I've ever had.

Happy Mother's Day to all moms everywhere. You are the most powerful, important people in the world.

Linda Goodnight

QUESTIONS FOR DISCUSSION

1. Discuss the main characters in this story. Who was your favorite? Why?

2. Carrie is sometimes embarrassed by her mother. Do you think that's typical of most mother-daughter relationships? Can you remember times when you were embarrassed by your own mother?

3. The Bible tells us to *honor* our father and mother. What does *honor* mean to you? Do you feel that Carrie honored her mother, even though they were so different? How?

4. Alzheimer's disease is a frightening diagnosis. Compare the differences in the way Frannie and Carrie handled the news. Did you think both were realistic? Why or why not?

5. How did Fran's beau, Ken, react to the news? Do you think this is a normal reaction? How did you feel about Ken after Frannie told him? Did your opinion change later on?

6. Have you or a loved one ever received a devastating doctor's report? How did you feel? How did those around you react?

7. Did the situation drive you closer to or farther away from God? Share the outcome and any insights you might have gained.

8. Discuss the difference in Carrie's view of God and Frannie's. Which is most like your walk with the Lord? Did either woman's journey deepen your relationship with God? How?

9. Carrie believes working within the church gives her brownie points with God. Does it? What is the role of "works" within the church? What does the book of James say about this?

10. At one point, Carrie considers withholding her church donations out of anger. Discuss this. Is it a common occurrence?

Is it right or wrong? What does Scripture say along these lines?

11. Talk about Carrie's secret sorrow concerning children. What was it? How does the Lord bring her full circle to fulfillment?

12. Discuss the symbolism of the airplane jump at the end of the book. How does it express Carrie's new freedom and faith?

13. Were you satisfied with the ending? Did it seem realistic, given the situation?

The employees of Thorndike Press hope you have enjoyed this Large Print book. All our Thorndike, Wheeler, and Kennebec Large Print titles are designed for easy reading, and all our books are made to last. Other Thorndike Press Large Print books are available at your library, through selected bookstores, or directly from us.

For information about titles, please call:
  (800) 223-1244

or visit our Web site at:
  http://gale.cengage.com/thorndike

To share your comments, please write:
  Publisher
  Thorndike Press
  295 Kennedy Memorial Drive
  Waterville, ME 04901